Published by Long Day Press
Chicago, Il 60647
LongDayPress.com
@LongDayPress

ISBN 9781950987108 (Paperback Edition)
ISBN 9781087931876 (eBook Edition)
Library of Congress Control Number: 2020951573

Edited by Joseph Demes & Joshua Bohnsack

Acknowledgements:
The following excerpts were previously published, "If You,
Too, Know the Words to 'Superbass'" in Joyland, "Night
Swim" in Necessary Fiction, as "Point of Transference," and
"Good Austin, Ninja Austin" in the anthology Teacher Voice
by Malarkey Books.

Printed in the United States of America
First Edition

Whimsy

a novella

SHANNON McLEOD

Long Day Press
Chicago

"*Whimsy* is lonesome and poignant, and even a bit funny, too. Shannon McLeod has written a moving, authentic portrait of a young woman at the start of her adult life, wrestling with its unfairness and unease. McLeod's heroine longs to be seen fully, and with compassion, but can't yet see herself that way, and it's compelling to watch her move through the world."

— Edan Lepucki, New York Times Bestselling Author of *California* and *Woman No. 17*

"Shannon McLeod's writing is funny, raw, and ultimately intimate and tender."

— Bryan Hurt, author of *Everyone Wants to Be Ambassador to France*

"In her tough and surprising debut novella, Shannon McLeod makes her nuanced observations feel inevitable. With steady restraint and immaculate pacing, rendered in only the simplest of strokes, it builds and builds to finally rupture so much greater than the sum of its parts."

— Tim Kinsella, author of *Sunshine on an Open Tomb*

"The women in Shannon McLeod's debut novella, *Whimsy*, are reminiscent of the women in Mary Miller's *Big World* and Roxane Gay's *Difficult Women*; young American women navigating a new world of female aloneness and autonomy, an aloneness in turns empowering and dizzying, battling society and men and themselves for feelings of self-worth and deservedness, battling the stillness of autonomy."

— Elizabeth Ellen, author of *Person/a: a novel*

Contents

If You, Too, Know the Words to "Super Bass"   9

Good Austin, Ninja Austin   25

Night Swim   39

Fred or Rick   51

What You Do Is   83

Adult Coloring   101

Skills   115

Passing Notes   135

Conferences   145

Bodily Expressions   155

Testing   165

If You, Too, Know the Words to "Super Bass"

I **know how human-interest** pieces work. I know
the series of emotions these stories take you through:
initial horror at the incident and the accompanying
images, then gratitude that the same did not happen
to you, and, finally, inspiration that the subject lives on.
As though simply existing were cause for admiration.

The journalist sat me beside my living room
window. He said the lighting was perfect. I imagined
the sunlight casting shadows along my scars. The burns
on my face and neck created ridges I did my best to
fill in with foundation. But the wrong angle revealed
every line. He'd discovered that angle. I wasn't sure
what sort of expression to make. Despite my nerves,
my natural inclination was to smile for a picture. Once
he lifted the camera, I remembered the type of article
the photo would accompany, and I relaxed my mouth,
squinted my eyes. He directed me to look into the far
corner of the room, sitting up straight.

"Straighter, please."

I suppose he wanted me to look stoic, brave.

Afterwards, he helped me move the chair and
coffee table back. I put my hand on his forearm and
asked if he'd like to stay for coffee. He hesitated before
saying yes. I wasn't sure if he was considering whether

it was a fake offer, asked out of politeness, or if he was feeling conflicted.

I can usually spot the look of internal struggle: when someone intends to be gentle to a person who is different, but not so gentle that it is obvious they are acting disingenuously. I decided he probably didn't want to stay, but he allowed his guilt to prevail. Maybe he hesitated out of the fear that I might be coming on to him.

I once had the luxury of negotiating attraction, of worrying I'd hurt another person's feelings. When an overweight classmate in high school asked me to come over for dinner after we stayed late at school working on a physics project, I made up an excuse. I wanted to be friends with him. He was the funniest kid in school. But the risk of leading him on if he wanted to be more than friends was more discomfort than I was willing to risk. Thinking back, I'm unsure whether I was more concerned about his discomfort or mine.

After my accident, the world grew incrementally more polite.

Maybe I was coming on to the journalist. Or I would have if he hadn't become so strange as we sat at my kitchen table with our coffee.

"Petrology is the area where I'm, you know, most interested right now, but I don't need to figure out my focus until next year, and it'll really depend on the lab opportunities. It all depends on a lot, so yeah."

Rikesh rambled on about his geology classes for his master's degree. We lived in Metro Detroit, where rock formations weren't exactly abundant.

"What's the point?" I asked. I wanted to know, and I also wanted to break him from his monologue. It was starting to grate on me that he was talking at me like this: like I was his senile grandmother who couldn't form a coherent response. I'd just given him an interview. He knew I could talk. Of course, during the interview he'd had his camera and laptop to distract him. He didn't have to look at me for sustained periods of time.

"What do you mean?" He looked up at my face for one or two seconds.

"I mean, why study geology?"

"Because I like rocks." He smiled, like it was cute that I was such an idiot.

I'd thought he was attractive when he first appeared at my apartment door. He had good bone structure, a wide jaw, and he stood tall. We were close to the same age. He might have been a few years older, late twenties or early thirties. But now, as he fumbled with my salt and pepper shakers and took tiny sips of his coffee in nervous succession, he began to appear pitiful, his character thin. I noticed the way his hair clumped in defined, gelled streaks.

Now he was talking about an archaeology camp he went to as a kid. I must have spaced out as he'd transitioned from discussing his classes to his childhood. His preferred topic of conversation was undermining his initial masculine impression.

The muffled sound of a vacuum cleaner came up from beneath the floorboards.

"What's that?" he asked.

"There's a vacuum store downstairs."

I got up and dumped the last of my coffee into the sink, cleared his mug off of the table. "You know, I forgot I told my mom I'd take her to an appointment," I said.

Rikesh nodded with polite understanding. He pushed back his chair and it made a scraping noise against the linoleum. He thanked me. He looked me in the eyes this time. I gave him a half-smile in return.

A while after he left, I called my mom. We talked on the phone every day since she moved away to Lansing to live with her new girlfriend, Barb. Soon *The Walking Dead* was coming on. We always watched it together with our phones at our sides set on speaker. As she told me about her day, I examined my face in the mirror. My foundation had nearly vanished—I touch my face when I'm nervous—and it must have happened during the interview. I could see my skin, the streaks of dark beige and reddish-white braided along my cheek. Frustrated, I pounded the cabinet beside the mirror. My mom didn't seem to hear the sound. She asked me what I was eating for dinner. I took a slow breath and wiped my eyes. I hadn't had anything to eat since breakfast.

I went to the fridge and examined its contents: bread, cheese, orange juice. The only produce left was a half of a lemon and a quarter of an onion, both in their own little baggies. I opened the cupboard and selected some cream of potato. Once it was heating on the stove, I sat down on the couch. Mom was talking about Barb's watercolor class. I heard a beep interrupt her, and I looked at my phone on the counter. It was Rikesh.

I told my mom I'd call her back and answered him. By now the soup was boiling, so I ran to turn off the burner. He spoke in that rapid-fire ramble he used when talking about himself over coffee. He said something about not having thanked me enough. I assured him that it was fine. I lied and said I was happy to do it. Then he asked me to dinner.

I shoved the pot of soup in the refrigerator. I texted my mom to tell her I had to answer more questions, and I wouldn't be able to watch the show. If I insinuated anything approximating a date, she'd be texting and calling all night.

I hadn't been on a date since Miri had set me up with her cousin, an amputee. We had "so much in common," she'd said. I didn't discover he was missing a hand until I arrived at the brewery. We ordered several flights of beer. I nodded enthusiastically as he told me more than I wanted to know about the difference between scotch ales, porters, and stouts—information I immediately forgot. I got drunk and embarrassingly giddy. I thought he was drunk, too, so I figured it was okay. The next day when I talked to Miri, who had already debriefed with her cousin, she reported that he had called me a "budding alcoholic." I remembered how tender I had felt towards him as I watched him struggle to open his wallet at the end of the date, fingers clutching one flap of leather while his stump pulled away the other. What an asshole.

I looked through my closet for something suitable. I wondered if it would be strange if I was wearing a different outfit when he picked me up. For the interview, I had dressed in slacks and a nice button-down shirt. If this were clearly a date, I would have permission to put on a dress. But I didn't know if it was a date. I decided to split the difference; I kept on my black collared shirt and traded my pants for a skirt cut just above the knee. In the bathroom, I applied a thick layer of foundation, blush, and powder. I still had half an hour until he would arrive. As the minutes passed, I paced my apartment. Each time I walked through my bedroom I put on another piece of jewelry. By the time he texted to say he was waiting out back, I jingled as I walked down the stairs.

Rikesh took me to one of those hibachi restaurants. I noticed when I got in his car that he was wearing the same t-shirt, but he'd replaced his puffy winter coat with a corduroy blazer. It felt somewhat serendipitous that we had both partially modified our outfits. During the car ride I wanted to ask him if his boss made him do it. If the editor told him he had failed to ask all of the most important questions, the personal ones. He failed to connect in the emotional way that a journalist must connect with his subject, especially if that subject was in an accident that killed two others, and the subject was the only one to escape alive. He failed to ask how it felt to walk around with evidence of that night all over her body.

"I just really wanted to show my appreciation for your time," he said as he opened the door for me.

The hostess asked if we wanted to sit at a grill or at a private table.

"Grill would be fun, wouldn't it?" He must have been asking me, but he addressed the question to the hostess. He rubbed the spot beneath his lower lip, like he was stroking a soul patch he didn't have.

I looked at the groups seated around the grills. On the other side of the room was the bar, surrounded by booths, which had curtains draped along their openings. "I'd rather sit at a booth." I didn't think I could handle worrying about the other occupants at the table staring at me while simultaneously navigating a conversation with Rikesh.

He asked me about what it was like to be a teacher. I told him I didn't have much to compare it to, but that it seemed I had less free time and less money than people with other careers. I was happy when he didn't respond with any platitudes about it being "rewarding."

"I was supposed to be teaching English in Africa

right now, actually." He draped his napkin over his lap.

"Oh?"

"My ex and I were planning on going into the Peace Corps together. But you have to be married if you want to be placed in the same country with someone." He opened his menu, as if that were the end of the story.

I looked at the dinner specials while I considered whether to push for more. I couldn't concentrate on the words in front of me until I asked. "So why didn't you get married?"

He lowered his menu just enough to show his eyes. "She didn't want to marry me." Then he raised the laminated page back up to hide his face entirely.

He asked how I felt about dumplings. I told him I felt very warmly towards them. When the waitress returned, he ordered the dumplings appetizer and a piña colada. I ordered a sake martini and promised myself it would be my sole drink of the evening.

After a few minutes of sipping and chewing, he broke our silence. "You did great with the interview. It can't be easy to talk about that." He swirled the straw around in his glass. "I think you're really brave."

"Brave?" I snorted and sipped my drink.

"Well, yeah." He chuckled nervously. "I'm a total coward."

When I'd first returned home from the hospital and refused to leave my bedroom, my mom told me to appreciate people for their good intentions, rather than chastising them for their poor execution. Then she made me go to Disney World with my aunt, who insisted on taking the whole family. After the trip, my aunt put dozens of photos on Facebook. She titled the album, "Celebrating Whimsy's Recovery." Her co-workers and friends I'd never met wrote comments, commending my aunt on her generous spirit.

"Me too," I said, trying to forgive his naivety. With my fingers, I combed the hair over the side of my face.

He asked if I wanted to ask him any questions about himself.

I chewed slowly as he watched me. It felt like it took extra effort to swallow while being observed. That familiar tightness in my chest took hold. I counted an inhale up to six. I counted an exhale to eight.

"I'm afraid I'll end up liking you too much, or otherwise I won't like you at all anymore," I said.

"You run that risk in any conversation, right? We're here to get to know each other. And I did just finish interviewing you. I thought you might like to turn the tables."

I looked around the room. The bartender was watching an ESPN recap on the TV above him. A group of teenage girls around a hibachi were applauding their chef.

"Okay, what I just said was mostly bullshit." I brought my gaze back to him. "I've been too busy thinking about my answers to the interview questions, analyzing how I must have come off and wondering what I can say to salvage your view of me."

He stuck out his lower lip, then shook his head. "Don't give me that much power. Let's just have a good time." The way he said it with authority, despite the modesty, made me feel comforted in his presence.

Our entrées arrived. We'd ordered three rolls to split, and I had my eye on the tempura shrimp roll. I reached over and plucked one off the platter with my chopsticks and transferred it straight to my face without a stop at my own plate. It wasn't until the sushi was crammed in my mouth that I realized this was improper. I looked around the room, hand covering my mouth while I chewed. When I looked back at him, he was staring at me. I thought he would look down, break our gaze after a few seconds, but he kept looking. Like he was contemplating me.

"Jane didn't like this place. She thought it was tacky, how it commodifies Japanese culture," he said.

"Sounds like the name of a girl who'd join the Peace Corps."

"What do you mean by that?"

"Safe, sweet. Like she needs some structured adventure in her life to make her feel like an interesting person."

"That's a bit judgmental," he said. He shifted towards the back of his booth. I'd thought we were banding forces by poking fun at Jane's privileged self-righteousness. Apparently, though, I wasn't allowed to play along in this game.

I didn't say anything in response. I didn't think I needed to apologize. I pulled the platter of shrimp sushi towards me and kept eating. I looked up as I lifted another piece to my mouth. He was grimacing.

"What?" I paused, mid-bite.

"You're eating the last one before I've had any."

"Oh, shit." I dropped it back onto the plate.

"No, no." He was laughing in earnest now. I noticed this was the first time I heard his genuine laugh, rather than his nervous one. "I'll order another plate of them."

"It'll make me feel like such a pig if you order another because I ate them all myself."

"But you *did* eat it all."

I studied the tablecloth.

"What if I eat the second one myself? Then we'll be even." He looked around for the waitress.

"Make sure the dish is in front of you. The plate cannot pass this soy sauce container," I said, drawing a line between us from the bottle to the opposite end of the table. "Otherwise I'll reach over and eat more without even realizing it."

The waitress returned, and he ordered another shrimp roll, along with another drink. I felt the hem of his pants graze my ankle, and my eyes drifted back to the TV. My muscles gripped my ribcage.

"You like sports?" he asked.

"Not in the least," I said.

"But it's more interesting than me."

"I guess so." I smirked.

He chuckled. I decided to forgive him for the slip up about his ex. Old love haunts us. Reminders trigger strange glitches in the brain. The second roll came out and he ate it all, like he promised.

Driving home, he turned the radio to the pop station I regularly listened to on my way home from work. I always made sure to keep my windows rolled up until I was a good mile away from the school, so my co-workers and students wouldn't discover my guilty pleasure.

He started to mouth the lyrics and tap his fingers against the steering wheel, mimicking the symphony of electronic champagne bottles popping. I thought it was time I paid him a compliment.

"I like that you seem to enjoy this music so shamelessly."

"Why should I be ashamed?" he asked without irony.

I watched as he continued to drum the wheel and softly sing.

"I think you're pretty uncool. But I like that about you. You seem to take pride in it," I said. We turned to each other at the same time and smiled, which made me blush. It felt so moronically precious. He slowed down and parked on the street. In the darkened storefront beside the car, the silhouettes of vacuums looked like people kneeling, praying, waiting to be taken home.

"Tell me more about rocks," I said.

He lowered his head so that he was looking up at me from beneath his dark, bushy eyebrows. "Would you want to check out my rock collection?"

I laughed. Then I realized he wasn't joking. He snorted in agreement with my laughter anyway. My hands began to shake. I said goodbye and got out of the car. I walked down the ice-slicked alley to the back of the building, where the steps led up to my apartment.

Immediately after closing and locking my door, he called me, asking if I had gotten inside safely. He thought there was a door at the front of the building, too, and he apologized for allowing me to walk down the alley alone. I told him I walked through that alley every day. I hung up, then worried I had sounded too defensive. Maybe it was meant as a gesture of kindness, and I had ended our interaction by pushing his kindness away.

I filled the bathtub and took a Xanax. I had held off on taking one all day. I had been trying to lower the frequency of my doses. My old therapist thought I was ready to try going without them altogether, which had been my idea, initially. I had been avoiding them during the daytime, but it was harder to deny the pharmaceutical help at night. Without it, I'd spend the next four hours staring at the ceiling above my bed, replaying conversations and praying for drowsiness.

In the tub, I tried to picture Jane. I wondered what he had been like in their relationship. I imagined him apologizing to her for something that shouldn't require apology. I tried to picture how we would be as a couple. Then I pushed these thoughts away. Too soon. I always let my mind go to these places too soon. Instead, I tried to focus on the feelings of bathing. The state of my mind as the drugs set in.

Anxiety is like getting out of the water, skin all wet. It only takes a slight breeze to inflict pain. I am sensitive and raw. The pills make me feel like I'm floating at the surface. Buoyed by the water, sensing it there, present, yet beneath me, while also feeling the fizz of blithe bubbles encasing my skin.

My phone sat on the bath mat, with the screen facing up so I could see if anyone—he—called. By the time the water was going tepid, it rang. The screen lit up, revealing my mother's name. I stayed put, listening to the ringtone until it went to voicemail. A few minutes later, she called again.

Good Austin, Ninja Austin

I don't know if you ever recover from the feeling of thirty pairs of eyes staring at you in concert. Especially when they're watching you during your first day on the job. Fortunately, it's not a feeling a teacher needs to get used to. By the third day of school only half of the students are paying attention at any given time. It's a relief once the pressure's off. By Halloween you're at the bottom of the students' lists of interests.

I was hoping no one would feel gutsy enough to joke about my face looking like a mask. So far, the students only seemed concerned with their own decisions about whether or not to wear costumes. I noticed them sizing each other up in the hallways. Most of the seventh graders hadn't worn costumes to school—they were too "mature"—but they would inevitably beg for candy from their younger siblings tonight. A few unfortunate ones assumed this year would be no different from sixth grade, when they marched alongside the kindergarteners in the Halloween parade. Angelo was dressed as a clown, with full makeup, a rainbow wig, and what must have been his dad's red Converse sneakers. He was dragging a stuffed dachshund behind him on a leash, grinning uneasily as his classmates laughed at him from the sides of the hallway. The clique of girls from the volleyball team all wore mouse ears. I watched Chanel draw whiskers on each girl's cheeks in front of her locker. Three of them were in my first period English class, where I'd intentionally split them up. Their assigned seats marked three corners of the room, so they weren't close enough to throw glances at each other when I'd make a pop culture reference they disapproved of.

The warning bell rang, and I left my hall duty post outside of my classroom door. I was convinced they'd given me (the newest hire) this room because of the location. Here, the hallway bent, and my classroom door was set in a semi-hidden alcove. Students used it for fights and make-out sessions. I had a broom by the door for when I needed to break up physical altercations.

Inside, the kids were already eating candy. Someone must have swiped a bag from their parents this morning because almost a dozen of them were gnawing on mini Snickers at their seats when the final bell rang, peanuts and crumbles of chocolate falling to their laps and onto the floor.

Austin W. sauntered in late, as usual, his backpack slung over one shoulder. The other day, I'd heard the department chair in the teacher's lounge say, "This year they're all named Austin. I can hardly keep track of all the Austins. A few years ago they were all named Hunter. Do you remember that?" The art teacher she'd been talking to nodded, her mouth full of noodles. And she was right. There were three in my first period alone. Austin W. was barely five feet tall. If a group of people were to approximate his age, I'd wager the average guess would be eight years old. He had a baby face, baby-thin blonde hair, and wore thick glasses that magnified his eyes. The first week of school, after I'd sent him to the office four days in a row, Judith, the vice principal, told me I had to start disciplining him in the classroom.

"He's just so cute that he gets away with murder," she'd said. "You need to show him he can't pull that crap."

Wasn't that her job? I'd thought. I was still learning.

Austin W. often talked to himself in an argumentative tone. I had a theory that he was trying to trick his classmates into thinking he had friends. Maybe he thought if he spoke aloud among groups, onlookers would think he was having a real conversation with someone nearby. A conversation where he was the intimidating one. Austin W. was wearing a ninja costume. One of the mouse girls made a crack about Power Rangers, and he responded by lunging his little hooded head towards her.

"Beat yer ass," he mumbled.

At the beginning of the year, it was alarming to witness an eight-year-old-looking child speak this way. Eventually, I learned to ignore it, like his classmates more or less had. I couldn't send him to the office for these offenses anymore. Until I figured out how to deal with them, I decided to pretend I had a hearing impairment.

As the students got out their grammar folders, I checked my phone. I spent so much class time telling students to put their phones away. I had to lodge my own between stacks of student papers on my desk so I could peek at it covertly throughout the day. The problem was, I'd pull the phone in and out from the papers so much that the paper's edges would get curled and crumpled. When I handed back the assignments, the pencil markings would be worn off from rubbing my phone's rubber case against them so frequently. It had been almost half an hour since I'd last checked. Still no texts from Rikesh.

I began my lesson on apostrophes, our daily grammar session. I was looking forward to getting this chore out of the way so that I could present the Halloween-themed creative writing prompt I had prepared as a special treat. I was excited to do something fun and festive with the kids. I'd written a short story inspired by a macabre illustration I'd found online. The plan was to turn the lights off and play the "Sounds of Halloween" screams track while I read the story, with the image of the old woman and her decapitated child projected on the board. After I modeled the activity for the kids, they would choose from a selection of other scary images and write their own stories.

On the board I wrote three sentences that needed apostrophes. The students copied them down, and I pulled out my phone again. Nothing. I looked across the room to check on Austin W. He sat at his corner seat closest to the door and karate chopped the air. In early September, I'd placed him in the front of the room. During my student teaching, my mentor advised me to put the troublemakers up front, so they would be more likely to focus on the lesson. But being at the front just meant Austin W. had the whole class as his audience. And it was harder to ignore him when he was up front. Now, I'd strategically placed him with two vacant desks surrounding him: one to the side and one in front of him. He was isolated, and that was the best I could do for classroom management. The student sitting kitty-corner to him was Austin G. ("Good Austin," as I called him in my head.) Austin W. leaned over and pretended to karate chop Good Austin's head. After a few slices of Austin W.'s hand through the air, Good Austin must have felt the slight breeze, because he swatted above him and the two slapped hands.

"*Heyyy,*" Good Austin whined as he swiveled around in his chair.

"Austin G., why don't you come up here and fix the first sentence on the board for me?" I said to distract from a potential hissy fit. He was always eager to show how good he was, so he walked up to the board, took the dry erase marker from my hand and added the apostrophes to the correct possessives and contractions. Next, I called on Jamar and then Sierra.

I instructed the students to put away their grammar and get out their journals. I turned off the lights and laughed maniacally. A few students giggled. Brody feigned a girly shriek, and laughter erupted. I put on the Halloween music and turned on the projector, revealing the gruesome illustration. In the low light, I could see the whites of most of their eyes, their attention rapt. I began to read my story, in a low, creepy voice. I got that giddy feeling in my abdomen, the rare sensation I felt when my lesson was going as planned and the students were all engaged.

"He was a bad little boy," I read in my creepy voice. "Each day, he woke his grandmother from her afternoon nap with some kind of prank." I looked up from my paper and scanned the students. Good Austin was turned around again, swatting away Austin W.

"Miss Quinn, Austin isn't supposed to be wearing a hood. No hoods or hats!" Good Austin called.

I walked down the aisle of desks, reading the next paragraph so as not to lose the attention of the other students. I kept glancing at the clock, hoping the students would have enough time to write their stories and share with partners.

"Miss *Quinnnn*," he whined.

I did not respond to Good Austin, but I paused my reading once I reached Austin W.'s desk. I leaned down and whispered, "You need to take off your hood, Austin."

He folded his arms and turned away from me quickly, like a toddler who hasn't gotten their way.

I read another sentence. At this point, all of the students had turned around. They were more interested in my feud with Austin than the decapitation of the little boy in the story.

I began to slide Austin's cherished Transformers lunchbox off his desk. "You can have this back when you take off your hood." He grabbed it and pulled back. I sighed and let go. The class's learning was more important than this, I decided. I walked back towards the board as I read the next sentence of the story, "Granny knew the way to teach the boy." I glared at Austin. I couldn't see his eyes, because his glasses reflected the light from the projector. I hoped he was looking. I hoped he could tell what I was communicating to him with my stare.

Then Austin W. lifted the lunchbox from his desk, raised his arm above his shoulder. His smirk spread into a grin, and he threw it. The lunchbox hit my shoulder. I heard gasps and a lone guffaw, probably Brody. I looked up at Austin, his glasses like little lasers below his polyester ninja hood. My face turned hot, my ears scalded. I reached down to pick it up. My arm began to throw it back towards him, but my brain interfered and instead I pulled my aim towards the floor. The tin lunchbox clattered against the linoleum. I saw Chloe speed from her chair to the back of the room. She took the emergency bathroom pass off the wall on her way out the door. I saw her ponytail flop down the hallway.

I decided to keep going. There was only one paragraph left in my story, and dammit if I would let Austin W. ruin my lesson plans. I heard whispers among the students. I cleared my throat and read louder, not realizing I'd ditched my theatrical voice. I was speeding through the story now. I had reached the point where the grandmother was tying a thin metal wire across the boy's play area, soon to call him in to build blocks with her. I looked back at the image on the board, remembering to read in my shrill old lady voice. "Come here, boy! Come *play* with me!"

The light flicked on. In the doorway stood Judith, her mouth agape. Chloe cowered close behind her. The class was silent. Only to be interrupted by a shriek from the CD player.

During lunch I walked down to the office. Judith wanted to see me. I hadn't spoken to the principal since he'd hired me, but I was becoming quite familiar with Judith. I felt the tension in my chest—which had become part of my regular bodily state since the school year started—pull tighter. As I approached the main office, I wiped my sweaty palms on my pants and opened the door. I peeked into Judith's office. She was eating fundraiser caramel corn from its plastic pail with one hand and typing an email with the other. Her desk was cluttered with decorative picture frames. They held several photos of her standing among groups of students: in the halls on "wacky hair day," in the gym at a basketball game, in front of the science center during a field trip.

Judith popped a kernel into her mouth and then held up one finger in the air. I took a seat at the small table. This was where she had her talks with students who'd been sent to her. Where I'd sent Austin W. on so many occasions.

I wondered about the likelihood that she would fire me. Maybe leave me home the rest of the week and dock my pay. I had fantasized about quitting, but I didn't really want to leave. Starting all over again would be a nightmare. If I could even find another teaching job.

My phone vibrated in my pocket. I pulled it out, instinctively, not thinking. It was Rikesh. I'd been waiting for him to text and here was a phone call.

"Is that an emergency or something?" I looked up from the screen to see Judith's left eyebrow hitched, taunting me. She had spun around in her office chair. Ready to confront me.

"Uh, no." I put the phone back in my pocket.

"This is the thing about teaching." She leaned back in her chair and it squeaked. "It needs to be the most important thing in your life. Otherwise, you'll be mediocre. Anyone can be a mediocre teacher. I don't want mediocre teachers here. Mediocre teachers do damage to children's development and harm their tenuous attitude towards school." She paused to inhale, then leaned towards me again. "Middle school is the make it or break it time when it comes to a child's relationship with education."

"Right, and I—"

She held her finger up again, and I shut up.

"Like I was saying, anyone can be a mediocre teacher. But it takes almost all your energy to be a great teacher. Because it takes up all your patience. All your commitment. If your mind, and your commitments, are elsewhere? You won't make it to year two."

That was it. A lecture. It had been enough for me, though. I left her office trembling, intent that I would do better, be better.

As I walked down the hallway, I fingered my cell phone in my pocket. I headed to the only single bathroom, tucked behind the band room. I'd gone here to cry enough times that I could no longer count them on one hand. I locked the door behind me. The light flickered—bright, then dimmer—making the tiles appear varying shades of yellowish, off-white. I carefully laid toilet paper on the seat and sat down. I heard the brass section on the other side of the wall: the buzzing of trumpets, the awkward sliding tone of the trombone.

I looked at my phone. It really was Rikesh who'd called. I was worried I'd imagined it or misread the screen during that quick glance in the office. He'd left a voicemail. My stomach felt like an elevator car. I remembered Judith's words, and, in an impulsive moment of self-punishment, I deleted it.

I felt what I thought was triumph. I could choose to be less selfish, to escape mediocrity.

The percussion section thundered a climbing drumroll. I placed my free hand against the tiled wall, feeling for the vibration. I imagined the instructor lifting his hands up, directing a crescendo. I pictured the students' eyes following him, all heeding his command.

I wiped my face with a damp paper towel, the scent of the recycled pulp like mulch. Lunch duty awaited me.

In the cafeteria, I stood by the trash can, directing students to pick up the balled napkins that had missed the rim. Then a pressure bore down on my head. I reached up to feel the thin plastic rim of a witch's hat. Judith was beside me, smirking. She smoothed out the tip, lifting it straight. "Show some Halloween spirit!" She shook my shoulder. "It's for the kids."

Night
Swim

We'd begun our tradition, Miri and I, once we were sixteen and old enough to drive. Miri's grandfather had an indoor pool, and we would go for a night swim on the evening before each of our birthdays. They weren't necessarily special—we used the pool at least once a month in high school—but it was important to us then to be with each other when we officially turned a year older. I hadn't felt close to Miri since high school, and maybe she hadn't felt close to me either, but we attempted to keep the tradition alive anyway, out of some shared sense of duty. After college, we both lost enthusiasm for the ritual. So it had been several years since we'd met at Miri's grandfather's to swim. I'd received her wedding invitation a couple months before and had been thinking about her in the weeks leading up to her twenty-fifth birthday. It's easy to remember the phone numbers and birthdays of your childhood friends. So difficult to remember anyone else's. Like your brain fills to capacity with those numbers growing up and won't tolerate fitting any more.

On a whim, I called her, asked if she'd happen to be around.

"I'm free that night."

• • •

It was nearing ten when she texted to say she was heading to her grandfather's house. Miri referred to it as a house, but it was really a mansion. When I arrived, she greeted me with a squeal. We gave each other a tight hug, rocking back and forth as we held onto one another to show how much we meant it. We said we'd missed the other. We asked when the last time we'd done this had been. We scolded ourselves for letting so much time pass. Filled with giddiness, I grabbed her hands and squeezed them.

I followed her into the downstairs dressing room, which she called a bathroom. It included three sinks, two stalls, a shower, and a Jacuzzi tub. Two benches mirrored each other on opposite sides of the room. This is where we'd go to change into our bathing suits, where we would sometimes smoke a pre-swim joint when we could get our hands on one.

I pulled my suit out of my bag. It was the first bikini I'd purchased in a decade. I usually hid the scars on my stomach. But over the past summer I read the autobiography of a British TV personality who'd had her face reconstructed after suffering sulfuric acid burns. It gave me the temporary courage to visit the mall and purchase the skimpy things I wanted to wear.

Miri got undressed quickly and without shame.

"What happened to your hair?" I asked.

She looked down at her crotch. It used to be natural, like mine. It had been familiar to me.

"William likes it this way," she said.

I fastened my top and watched Miri look over her reflection.

"So, I got us some of that wine we used to love." Miri pulled up her bottoms.

"What's that?"

"White Zinfandel." She winked. She could pull off winking.

When we got to the pool, Miri walked in from the shallow end, holding her lungs full, like the warmth of her breath would protect her from the water's chill. I did a cannonball into the deep end. It's the only way I've ever been able to get into the water.

I swam towards Miri. Her body looked even more incredible than it had in high school. I wanted to say so, but wasn't sure how to put it in a way that wouldn't sound strange or envious. As teenagers, I'd developed first, and she was the one who'd been jealous of me— even though I was too shy to talk to boys then. And she'd always been better at getting boyfriends.

Miri bent her knees to briefly dunk herself up to her shoulders.

I wanted to revive our old banter, but I stayed silent. It seemed like Miri was thinking of something else, anyway.

I dove down and swam in a circle. Underwater, my skin looked smoother, tinted a pale green. My hair floated in front of my face as I took a sharp turn.

The strands became copper colored in the pool light. My legs drifted and kicked. They looked sleek, strong, useful. For a moment I felt beautiful.

When I came up for air, I flipped onto my back and looked at the ceiling as I did slow backstrokes. I wasn't ready to see Miri, to feel ugly by comparison. In my mind I tallied up all the men who had seen me naked. Only one had been with my bare body since the accident. On a weekend stay at my dad's the summer after my sophomore year of college, Dad invited his work friends over for a party. After the bonfire had died down and the others had gone home, or found a place to crash inside, Philip and I were left sitting on the lawn chairs. He'd brought his camper so he could pass out drunk in the backyard. I was adamant about keeping my shirt on, the lights off. He became instantaneously sober long enough to turn on the light, to talk me out of my clothes. He ran his hands over my hips and I closed my eyes.

Across the pool, Miri was still standing in the shallow, the water level just above her navel. She swept her palms against the surface of the water. The lights from the bottom of the pool shone on her face, casting wiggling lines across her forehead. Even Miri's posture seemed different; her limbs moved more stiffly. I tried to remember the last time I'd seen her. It couldn't have been more than eight months ago. Yet she had found a way to change everything about herself. Could I change that quickly too, if a man asked it of me? All of our beliefs that we'd shared, the things I thought were inherent in ourselves and made us special, turned out to be so malleable.

I dove down again, pulled the water beside me until I reached the shallow edge. I did a careful flip beside her and pushed myself back towards the deep end. I quickly found the bottom and my stomach scraped lightly against the gritty concrete. On the thin tissue of my stomach, I could almost feel the tiny abrasions that were cut into my skin. It felt good, like plucking a deep-rooted hair from a knuckle, like holding a palm to a candle flame. I planted my hands on the bottom of the pool and shoved hard, anxious for breath. I treaded water for a moment and looked up at the wall facing me. On it there was a window that looked out into a hallway. The only lights, besides those along the inside edges of the pool, came from that window. In the near dark, the hall light was so bright that I hadn't yet noticed the mural on the wall beside the window. It hadn't been there before. It looked like a Picasso rip-off: strange angular faces floated just above bodies, which were depicted through blue and green boxes. Some of the figures had mouths with teeth jutting out in yellow triangles, pink squares. Others had no mouths. It started to scare me, so I turned around.

Miri was out of the water, sitting on a vinyl-upholstered couch, one piece in the set of patio furniture that lined the opposite end of the pool. I swam towards her, my mouth grazing the surface of the water. She pulled the bottle of wine out of her handbag and set it on the couch between her legs. I got out of the pool and picked up a towel from the bin beside the furniture. The bin was always stocked, like a nice hotel. Whenever we'd come here to swim, I'd catch myself looking out the window any time I took a towel. I thought her grandfather might come rolling down the hallway and yell at me to drop it. He never did. I only ever saw him when we said hello to him upstairs as we first arrived—unless it was night. Then we would slip inside quietly. Once in the pool, our voices would grow louder. The echoes of the tile-lined room and our increasing inebriation amplified our shouting.

I pulled the towel around my shoulders and dried myself off, moved down to my legs. Then I wrapped the towel around my head. I sat next to Miri. She was screwing a bottle opener into the cork. She pulled it open with a pop that rang out to the walls and reflected back into our ears, bouncing again and again. It was the first echo we'd heard that night.

"I wonder if there are any cups around here," Miri said. She knew there weren't. I didn't know why she had asked.

"Let's just drink from the bottle," I said. It had never been a problem before. I grabbed it from her hand and took a swig. The sweetness tasted of aspartame. I looked at the label for ingredients and found only a description of the notes of strawberry and thyme, wafts of cinnamon. My shoulder was touching hers. One of us must have been shivering because our goosebumps began to rub up against each other. I passed her the bottle. "That's pretty sick, but I think it's the kind of sick that gets better as you drink it."

She snorted. I interpreted it as mild laughter. She sipped from the bottle, set it on her thigh, and then sipped again.

I grabbed the corkscrew from her lap, and she flinched. It was red with white lettering. "Aestetica," I read aloud. "What's that?"

"William's graphic design company."

"He owns it?"

"He only became VP a couple years ago."

I reached out for the bottle and she handed it to me. "And he's how old?"

"Fifty-two."

I was about to say, "Old enough to be your father." I figured she had heard that before, or at least thought it, so I took another drink instead.

"He's very youthful, though." She took back the bottle and stood up. "You should meet him."

"I'd like to," I said. I followed her to the edge of the pool. I had the urge to push her in. I wanted her to scream and shriek. I wanted us to laugh together. But I had a feeling it would just make her angry. So I put my arm around her waist. After a moment, she put her arm around my shoulder and patted it. She let her hand drop to her side, so I let mine drop down, too.

"Do you want to play a drinking game?" I asked, grabbing the bottle from her hand.

"Like what?"

"Like..." I looked around the room, which was occupied by only the pool, the patio furniture, and the hideous faces behind us. "Like a relay. You have to swim a lap, staying underwater as long as possible. For every breath you come up for, you have to take a swig. Then when you're done, I go."

"Sounds like a recipe for vomit."

"I can't believe I haven't already from this stuff." I sat down and put my feet into the water. I shivered. I took a sip.

I told her I was getting tired, and she didn't plead for me to stay any longer. I dried my hair off with the towel. We changed back into our clothes. I put on my jacket and pulled the hood over my head.

"Are you staying here tonight?" I asked.

"Yeah. I'll just crash in one of the guest rooms."

"Oh." I said, waiting for her to invite me to do the same, as she'd done in the past. When she didn't, I asked, "What are you doing for Thanksgiving?"

"William's coming here for dinner. My grandfather wants to meet him. He is paying for the wedding, so he wants to make sure he approves of him first." Miri hadn't yet put her pants back on. She was in her blouse and thong, squirting lotion into her palm.

"When's the wedding again?"

"Whimsy! Didn't you get the invitation? It's next month!" Her eyes were gaping wide.

I'd put the invitation in a drawer where I wouldn't have to look at it every day.

"I've always wanted a winter wedding, and William didn't want to wait a year and a half when he proposed." She smiled to herself, smoothing the lotion onto her legs, and reminded me of the date. She looked beautiful, like herself. Behind her in the mirror, I could see my reflection. The scars on my face were hardly visible under the shadow of my hood. I tried to remember our conversations, years ago, about marriage. We must have talked about it. It seemed like all we did was discuss our opinions on relationships. I couldn't remember any specifics, though. Now that we were actually living it, I supposed it didn't matter what we used to think about adulthood.

I wished her a happy birthday and assured her I'd be at the wedding. I went in for a hug. The air in my puffy jacket seeped out as I squeezed her, this girl that I loved so much and could no longer talk to.

On the drive home, I blasted the heat. It was after midnight; most of the stoplights had turned to blinking yellows, blinking reds. Though there was hardly anyone else on the roads, I kept below the speed limit. Patches of black ice would have sprung up in the potholes. I had been drinking, but I didn't think a person could be fated for two car wrecks in one lifetime. I could drive this route in my sleep.

Fred
or
Rick

Mostly, what I remember of the accident is colors and sound. Tara's funeral is a blank, filled in with imaginings. What I remember clearly is the wake: sitting in an armchair in the corner of her parents' living room with a family photo album, focusing on the pictures to make a shield between me and the dozens of unfamiliar, sweaty bodies milling around. I had just been released from the hospital. Every time I got up or sat down or walked around, the bandages chafed and some new, painful sensation emerged. My right arm was immobile, strapped and bent in front of my torso. One foot was in a walking cast—a "robo boot," as the nurse called it. I decided to stay put.

It seemed like a nice house. Her family upheld a welcoming attitude despite their grief. It made me wonder why Tara had chosen to live in the dorms when she had this kind of home just twenty minutes from campus.

I had been excited about having a roommate at college. I was an only child, and I thought this might make up for missing the camaraderie of a sibling. But things began awkwardly. When I arrived on move-in day, her things already filled up half of the room. Her bed was claimed with a hot pink blanket.

Her furniture was situated against the wall with the window. Her half of the room was brighter; my side looked sad, all white and bare. I hadn't had any say in the arrangement, though it was nothing that could extinguish my excitement. But that night, when I imagined we might try scouting out a party, she sat me down. I immediately worried I'd done something wrong, even though it hadn't been six hours since I'd moved in.

"I've had—have—anorexia." Her face looked grim when she corrected herself.

I nodded.

"I was wondering if you might just keep an eye on me? Like, say something if you notice I stop eating?"

I nodded more vigorously. In my chest, panic bloomed.

She smiled and seemed to relax. "I usually have my brother to help with this."

After that, I sought out friends from other rooms on our floor. But they'd somehow already found time to establish cliques. Tara spent all her time in the room on the phone with her boyfriend. Most evenings I'd lay in my bed, looking at the ceiling, pretending I couldn't hear her conversations. I could determine if she would be happy or depressed after the call based upon the intonation with which she said the word, 'babe' over and over. If it was a particularly whiny series, I'd put on my headphones and crank up my music. I hated to hear her cry.

I had only known her for a month. Going to the

concert was supposed to get us out of the dorms, together. I'd been the one who was driving.

"You're Tara's roommate." Her brother approached with a plastic cup held out in offering. "Care for some social lubricant?" He sat on the loveseat perpendicular to me. We'd never met, but I recognized him from her photos. He recognized me by the bandages on my face. I sniffed the cup. Whiskey? Or bourbon? At the time, I didn't understand the difference.

"I can't drink with my medication." I held it back out to him. "I'm really sorry about your sister."

We sat for a moment in silence. Then he pointed to the open page of the photo album in my lap. "Mackinac Island," he said. "Have you been?"

"Just once. My mom thought it was lame."

"What did you think?"

"I was little. I liked the horse-drawn carriages. And the fudge." I turned the page and stole a glance at his reaction to the next picture: his family standing in front of the Grand Hotel. He blinked his eyes rapidly. He had freckles, like his sister.

"Tara ate so much fudge on that trip she had this stomach ache all weekend. My parents called it a fudge hangover."

I laughed quietly and waited to see if he would smile.

An older couple stopped in front of him. They each put a hand on one of his arms. The woman began to cry.

"Have you seen these pictures yet?" Tara's brother

reached over and lifted the photo album from my lap, handed it to the older gentleman. He stood up and invited them to sit on the couch with the photos. At my side, he leaned down and spoke quietly, "Do you want to see my room?"

I hobbled down the stairs behind him. In the basement, he led me past a small kitchenette across from a TV and couch and opened the door to his bedroom. He sat on one end of his bed. I sat on the other. The only additional piece of furniture was a chair, piled high with laundry. There were framed Detroit Pistons posters on two of the walls, a cheap-looking bookshelf on another. The fourth wall contained two doors—a closet and a bathroom, I figured.

"Is this whole basement yours?"

"Moved down here after high school." He pulled a pack of cigarettes from his bedside dresser drawer and held it out to me. I shook my head. "Do you mind if I…?" he asked. I shook it again. I wondered if he could get away with smoking in his parents' house if the circumstances were different.

"What's your name?" I asked. "I'm so sorry, I forget." It was likely on the funeral program. Tara must have mentioned it a few times, too.

He took a drag on his cigarette. Then he said what sounded like Fred or Rick, his voice obscured by smoke.

"Fred or Rick?" I asked.

He laughed. "Frederick. But, yeah, most people call me Fred."

"Can I call you Rick?" It felt reckless, being flirtatious after a funeral. But one only had so much energy, and when it had to be used for physical recovery there wasn't much left for neuroticism. Since the accident, my usual obsessive dissection of conversations in my head had become muted—at least temporarily.

"Can I call you Zee?" he said, and smirked.

He must have been a good brother, I thought, to know such things about his sister's life as small as her roommate's name.

He went to Western Michigan, too, and was two years ahead of us, studying sports medicine. But his real dream, he told me, was to become a comedian. By the time I began telling him about myself, we heard footsteps coming down the stairs. He stubbed his cigarette into a mug. His mother appeared in the doorway. She ignored me and asked Frederick to come upstairs to say goodbye to his uncle. She said nothing of the smell.

Two weeks later I got a phone call from an unknown number. I was propped up in my bed, underlining things I guessed might be important in my psychology textbook. The lines I made were shaky. It looked like I was crossing things out.

"It's Fred."

"Who? Oh, *Rick*. Hi."

"Huh, yeah. Listen, we're coming to pick up Tara's things today. Feel free to be in the room, but I thought you might feel awkward about it without a heads-up."

I assured him I'd be out within the hour. After I'd saved his number in my phone, I shut the book and looked around the room. It was so abrupt. After the funeral, I had made a strange effort to get to know my roommate better and started going through her things. In the top drawer of her dresser, next to a neat stack of ankle socks and a small cloth container of her underwear, I found another container, filled with junk that could find no proper place: purple lip gloss in a tube shaped like a teddy bear, faded friendship bracelets made of embroidery floss, a deck of Detroit Tigers themed playing cards, and an envelope filled with photographs. There was one of Tara and Frederick standing in line at an amusement park. Tara must have been wearing Frederick's baseball cap. It looked too large and oddly placed on her head, so that strands of hair were pulled across her forehead. I imagined Frederick setting it on her head and twisting it before the picture was taken. I had set this photo on my dresser next to my bed.

I'd known this would happen, but I hadn't prepared myself. I had turned off the daily seven AM alarm that was set on her bedside clock. I had washed the clothes in her hamper and returned them, neatly folded, to her dresser drawers. But I hadn't thought much about her stuff going missing from the room, for all traces of her to disappear.

I went downstairs for an early dinner. It was just

after four o'clock, and the cafeteria was nearly empty. I was still moving slowly, my muscles regaining strength. It was a comfort to not feel rushed, without crowds of students behind me. I took my time browsing the hot bar. Nothing looked appetizing, so I toasted a bagel and assembled a plate of salad. Sitting beside the window, I opened my copy of *Middlemarch*. My professor had excused me from the required paper, but warned that the book would be addressed on the midterm exam. I ate one bite per page, stretching out my time in the cafeteria, feeling grateful that I'd opted for a meal that could be eaten cold. It felt leisurely, even though it—and everything else—was catch-up work.

But I soon became distracted from my reading. Maybe I should have offered to help Tara's family, I thought. Maybe I should have asked to keep something of hers. I may not have known her well, but I still felt I wanted something to hold onto. She was my roommate; she could have been my friend. I didn't want to return to the room feeling completely abandoned. Still, I re-focused and continued to read.

Once I finished my meal, I'd read thirty-two pages. Only an hour and a half had passed since I'd left the room. I brought my tray to the dishwashing area and helped myself to a bowl of ice cream. More people were beginning to enter the cafeteria now. Two girls who sat at the table behind me were discussing whether they should join a dance team. I gave up on reading for a bit and eavesdropped instead, looking out the window at the slow-moving branches.

One of my fears was that my body would always remain in the frail state it reached during my hospital stay. It began before Tara died. She was in the ICU, but, for some reason, I assumed she would be fine. During that week before her death, I spent my energy focusing on the horrifying medical subterfuge of having my skin grafted and relocated to my face, the withered look of my legs on the bed in front of me. After she died, I remained focused on my body. I now considered whether this was a coping mechanism. I didn't know her that well. But I still thought of how another girl would be wrecked by the loss. I felt more guilt, more disgust with my body than loss. And recognition of these feelings compounded the guilt, which I tried my best to bury. I told myself that when I got out I would need to stretch my legs, build my muscles—make my body more alive again. I started walking along the trails, winding between university buildings. I had heard stories of the nearby forest, of rape, so I avoided the paths that led to the woods.

After I had sat as long as I could stand it in the cafeteria, I went outside. I walked slowly around a neighboring dormitory. The sun was setting, and I could see more clearly into the rooms that had their lights on: girls straightened their hair in preparation for evening activities; boys played video games. In one room, I saw the faint outline of a head bobbing around in front of a guy's crotch. He held his arms above him like he was yawning. I fingered the side of my face. I wasn't supposed to touch the still-healing wound, but I grabbed my cheek at times when I didn't mean to.

There was a bench ahead. The street light beside it had just turned on. I sat down and got the book out of my purse. I tried to read, but in my peripheral vision stood the woods. I glanced over every so often. I hadn't seen any girls walk down the forest path since I'd sat down. I thought about if anyone was waiting among the trees, if they might grow impatient and search the outskirts. And I thought about myself: sitting alone, visibly injured. I stood up and checked the time on my phone like I had somewhere to be, someone to meet.

I went into my dorm through the back entrance. Once I finally reached the third floor, I walked through the hallway slowly, listening for Tara's family. If I noticed they were still here, I decided, I would go back downstairs to the common area and continue reading. My door was closed. I put my ear to the surface and heard nothing. Inside, half of the room's contents were gone. I looked out the window and saw a van pulled to the side of the drive. Tara's mother was already seated on the driver's side. Frederick put a cardboard box in the trunk and lowered the hatch. Her father stood with his back to the passenger door, took off his glasses, and pinched the bridge of his nose. On my dresser I found the picture among my own scattered possessions. The photo was face down. I couldn't remember if I had left it that way.

What I still don't know is whether I wanted

Frederick to love me as a measure of absolution. It makes sense that I'd want reassurance. I had gazed at my blind spot a second too long. When I looked back in front of me, we were halfway into the next lane. In my startled state, I over-corrected. It was rainy. I jerked again to over-correct the over-correction. We spun out. An oncoming car T-boned us. I wasn't even conscious to witness her body being crushed. I feel guilty for that, too. I never had to see anything, until it was the chrome and white and gray of the hospital. I didn't see the colors of gnarled flesh until I had to confront my own.

The next day I had a psych test. I had tried my best to prepare despite missing the lectures on the unit, but there were questions about terms and studies that I swore weren't anywhere in the textbook. Afterwards, I felt the need to hole up in my room, and call my mom, before I could brave the crowds of students at dinnertime. The week before, two frat boys cornered me at the pop dispenser and asked about my face. They expressed concern in a tone that I couldn't quite pin as sarcastic or genuine. But when I took my usual seat by the window, I couldn't keep myself from imagining them laughing about me at their table, comparing my skin to their lunch meat. I didn't have the fortitude to deal with something like that again. When I opened the door to my room, I noticed a figure on my bed. I screamed. A door a few rooms down opened, and my

RA barreled out to the hallway.

"Whimsy, it's just me." Frederick stood up from the bed and took steps towards me.

I clutched at the doorframe and tried to breathe. I turned and told my RA it was just a prank, no big deal. She mouthed, "Okay" and returned to her room.

He sat back on my bed. I noticed his eyes, rimmed in pink, underlined in a grayish purple.

"My mom asked me to return Tara's key."

I should have been angry, scolded him for intruding. Instead, I took a seat in front of Tara's now-empty desk. He moved to my chair. My silence must have spooked him.

"Sorry," he said. "I just wanted to hang out."

Frederick should have resented me—hated me, even—given the circumstances. But here he was. So I told him about the test. Rick offered to give me his notes from his freshman year psych course. There was an open mic at the comedy club that night, he said and asked to practice his set. He stared at the wall behind me for a while, and then began his jokes. I tried to laugh at the right times, but it was a lot of pressure being the sole audience member. The jokes were mostly about girls he'd dated. One started the same as a dozen set-ups I'd heard before. He said he accidentally called a woman the name of an ex. Then she called him Joe Pesci for a month in retaliation. Frederick's jokes made me wonder if he had a girlfriend. It sounded like he juggled a lot of women.

But maybe that's just how he wanted it to sound.

Frederick asked me for feedback. I didn't know anything about comedy, so I referred back to what I knew from having danced. I suggested he make better use of the stage.

"What do you mean?"

"Move around more. Make gestures to emphasize what you're saying."

He invited me to the show. I hesitated, and then said I had to catch up on schoolwork.

The next day he called to tell me his set went well. People laughed. Frederick heckled a girl in the front row for wearing see-through leggings that showed her underwear, and her boyfriend got angry and threatened him. "It was awesome," he said. I congratulated him. He asked if he could come over.

Half an hour later, there was a knock, and moments after, he peeked his head around the door. I closed the window on my laptop where I'd been watching a TV show aimed at thirteen-year-old girls. He sat beside me on the bed. From his pocket he pulled out a plastic baggie and a one-hitter painted to look like a cigarette. I worried how the weed would mix with my pills. When I voiced this concern, Frederick said he'd smoked while on painkillers before.

"It was awesome," he said, his refrain.

I took two hits and said I was done. It was much stronger than anything I'd smoked before. Pretty soon I felt I could barely keep my eyes open. He begged me to come to his stand-up performance next week. I agreed this time.

"Do you need new material?" I asked him.

Frederick was scrolling through the music on my computer. "Huh?"

"I made up a joke."

"What is it?" He looked up from the screen.

I started laughing at it—the stupidity of my joke. It took a while to stop giggling and gather my composure. "Okay." I inhaled deeply. I stared him in the eyes and forced my face into a solemn expression. "*Ruthless?* Ruthless is my middle name. Actually, it's just *not* Ruth."

Frederick burst out laughing. He curled up on his side and rolled from the bed onto the floor. Even in my state I could tell he was doing this for my benefit. But I didn't care. I kept laughing along with him.

He asked if he could try out my joke on the crowd. I nodded as I took a swig from my bottle of water. He pulled it out of my hand and took a sip. From the hallway we could hear the familiar high-pitched squeals of college girls.

"She gets a whole double room to herself now," one said.

"That is *so* not *fair*," the other went.

Before the open mic, Rick and I stopped for dinner at a place called Soup, Soup, Soup! We sat by the window beside a table of nurses. The woman who sat facing me wouldn't stop staring. She had dyed red hair styled so that the front was plastered to the sides of her cheeks and the back was spiked up. I tried to focus on my sandwich, on Frederick, but I couldn't help looking back to check if she was still staring at me. I thought it a look of disgust, or resentful exhaustion, as she slurped her tomato soup and stared at my face.

It was getting colder outside. I wore my walking cast on one foot and a winter boot on the other. Only my left arm could bend through the sleeve of my winter jacket, the other was pinned against my chest. As we walked from the restaurant to the venue, Frederick kept flipping my empty right sleeve with his hand. Then he grabbed the wrist of the sleeve, like he was holding my invisible hand, and swung the sleeve back and forth.

What I liked best about Frederick was that acting like a fool didn't embarrass him; he seemed to enjoy himself even more when in public. It put me in a lighter mood. It kept me distracted from the pain in my leg as I walked.

He insisted we get to the comedy club early, so he'd get an open mic slot. I found a table while he signed up. I watched him from across the room as he chatted with the bearded man who guarded the sign-up sheet. Then he walked to the bar and returned with two pints of beer.

"I shouldn't drink," I said, slightly annoyed, as he set them on the table.

"And you shouldn't smoke either, but you did and you were fine." He stared at me, his eyebrows raised, until I picked up the beer and drank.

Frederick told me he'd had to negotiate with the manager to go last. But no one ever wants to go last, or first. I sipped the beer slowly, cautiously. By the time he took the stage I was nearly finished and my stomach was flipping. At first I told myself it was the sandwich, then I decided it was just anxiety. I heard him use the "ruthless" bit, but by that point I could feel the hot, acidic trickle up my throat, taste the salty flush inside my mouth. I ran to the bathroom. I waited a while afterwards, to make sure I was really finished, before emerging from the stall. I rinsed out my mouth and drank water from the faucet.

The lights in the club had been raised slightly and Frederick was off the stage, standing at a high-top table with four young women. His arm was around the shoulders of one. She wore too much eyeliner. I fished a piece of gum from my purse and sat at our table, considered whether to join them. I didn't have to introduce myself if I didn't feel like it, I thought. I watched as the girls all grinned at him. He was reciting an anecdote—I couldn't hear from the table, but I could tell from the way he moved as he talked—and relishing the attention. They all burst into laughter at the same time.

I went to the bar and ordered a glass of ice water. When I returned, Frederick was in my seat.

"Where'd you go?"

"Bathroom. I told you I wasn't supposed to drink," I said and sat down. I couldn't keep my gaze from following the group of girls traipsing towards the exit. "Who're they?"

"Ooh, jealous, aren't we?"

I rolled my eyes and inadvertently touched my cheek.

"They're in my kinesiology class."

"They seem *happy*," I said, staring him down.

"They wanted to come to a show."

"That's great." Heat rose to my face. I exhaled, trying to rid myself of it.

Frederick walked me back to my dorm and followed me up to my room. I didn't invite him in, and he didn't ask if he could come in. I thought of the room key he still had and held the door open behind me so he could slip inside.

He opened my laptop and put on Nick Drake while I took off my boot and my cast. We sat on my bed and looked at the opposite side of the room. We didn't talk for a long time. I felt the bed shift as he turned towards me. He put his hand on my face. I flinched as I felt his fingers trace the place where my stitches had recently been removed.

"I'm sorry," he pulled his hand away.

"I can barely feel a thing."

He was careful as he kissed me. I leaned in closer. He lowered his hand, pulled it away from me, as I kissed his neck. His hand reappeared on my low back and snaked its way under my shirt. I pulled away.

"Please, don't touch me there," I said.

He stood up and unzipped his pants. I grabbed him and did what came next. I rushed towards it without question. He seemed to be doing the same. I wondered if his arms were held over his head, like the guy I saw through the window, but I didn't want to look up.

Afterwards, I asked him to lie down with me. I was supposed to lie only on my back, but I turned onto my left side to make room for him on the twin bed. He stood for a while before he joined me. The bed felt bigger, somehow, with both of us in it, with the way he found space enough to keep his back from touching my abdomen. I placed my arm over him. I hoped to signal that he could come closer. He must have been afraid of hurting me.

"It's okay," I said. "Just don't lean your weight on my collarbone."

He didn't move or speak. I thought he might have been dozing off. I left my arm over him, but it felt strange. It looked like something that didn't belong there, like a rubber hose draped over a birthday cake.

"I'm sorry." He pushed himself up off the bed and stood. "I don't have a lot of friends." He sighed, "Basically just my parents, now." It sounded rehearsed, his self-pity. He looked up at the wall, where his sister had once placed a whiteboard to write herself reminders and due dates. "I want you to be my friend."

I pushed myself upright and planted my feet on the rug, pulled my free arm over the slinged one.

"What about your friends from the show?" I snapped.

He looked back at me. "Those are just girls. *You're* my friend."

It was a cheap shot. I crossed my legs and looked at my feet. I'd been practicing walking without the robo boot, up and down the halls. It was strange for my legs to be the same length again, without the lift of the cast under my right foot. My hips and back hurt as the result of hobbling around on uneven legs.

"I'd like my room key back." I looked up at him. He was staring at the wall again. It seemed we both had the habit of shutting down when things didn't go the way we'd planned them in our heads.

"It's Tara's key."

"It's my room," I said steadily.

He jutted out his jaw. This gesture looked familiar: the expression a person makes before they start swinging. He pulled his wallet from his back pocket and lifted the key from it. I looked away when he held it out to me.

I would stare at Tara's bed. I remembered her that night, sitting on her pink comforter, which was now removed, exposing a thin mattress encased in a protective vinyl material. I remembered her asking me to look out for her, and how even that was too great a request for me to handle. It occurred to me that this might be why I didn't have friends. But when epiphanies came at night, I never had enough energy for action. I'd always felt more emotionally unstable in the evening. I wondered if that was the case for Rick.

The next day, I tried to forget about it all. But there was no way to avoid replaying every event of the previous night. By the evening, I decided to go see him. I would apologize. Maybe get an apology in return. It was two AM. I managed to catch the last bus to his side of town—the drunk bus, as they call it. The only open spot was in the back, where the seats were situated in a U-shape. Out of habit, I looked out the window, but with the darkness outside, and the artificial light inside the bus, all I could see was my face: wrecked and ugly. I turned my gaze to the floor, studied the wrappers and empty cans rolling around between the passengers' feet. Next to me, a group of guys taunted one another about not getting any.

I could feel staring. I felt it often. Usually when I turned, no one was looking. Merely looking past me. But when I turned towards the feeling, one guy—freckled and wearing the anonymous gray sweatshirt the university gave to all incoming freshmen—was staring at me. His mouth hung open, head swaying with the bus's movement.

"What's…" he mumbled.

This time I didn't slink away. "What are you saying?" I barked.

He cleared his throat. "What's wrong with your

face?" He squinted and moved closer to inspect me. "What happened to you?"

The more lucid members of his posse turned their attention to our interaction. They asked one another what he'd said, trying to sound as though they thought they were whispering. It was more like raspy shouting.

"Brian just asked that chick what's wrong with her face," another guy said, his voice low and slow. They all laughed in the same itchy, stoned pitch.

"Fuck off." I pulled the cord and stood. I walked back home from there.

The next day I drove to my mom's apartment. I arrived unannounced. She made me pancakes as I told her about the modern dance group that I hoped to join when the season started in the new year.

"Don't overdo it," she said. "You better ask the doctor."

"I won't. And I will. I just need something to look forward to."

She delivered a plate of lopsided cakes to my placemat.

For the next several weeks, I threw myself into school. I met my professors during office hours to make sure I was doing everything I could to keep my grades up. My bandaged, cast-covered presence played into their sympathies. They all cut me varying degrees of slack. I didn't see Frederick. He texted me, but I declined his invitations to coffee. I wouldn't know what to say to him.

I passed my classes. After first semester, I spent two weeks at my mom's apartment. I set up and decorated our miniature artificial tree. I visited my dad and convinced him to drive us to the local church's parking lot to pick up a real tree. I thought about Frederick. I thought about how hard Christmas must be for him, the first year without his sister. I texted Miri about seeing a movie. After an hour without hearing back from her, I called Frederick.

When he picked up, I closed my bedroom door. I wrapped myself in a blanket and sat on my bed. "What'd you get for Christmas?" I asked him in a shaky voice.

"Some Tonka trucks. How about you?"

I made a conscious effort to lower my shoulders. I hadn't been sure if we could go back to this banter again. "An easy bake oven," I said.

"Are you going to bake me a cake when you get back to your dorm?"

"Hell no." I said. "Those mixes are like five bucks a pop. I'm not wasting one on you."

He chuckled.

I waited in silence for a few moments. I was relieved he was playing along. I didn't want to feel uncomfortable anymore. I had moments when I couldn't uphold the self-punishment. Without Frederick, I walked among the crowds on campus with this endless looping thought: *Nobody knows me.*

"Are you okay? This time of year brings up a lot

of grief." I said it just how I'd thought it. Aloud, the phrase sounded stilted and wrong.

"Um."

"I'm sorry. If you don't want to talk about it, we don't have to."

After a few moments, he broke the silence. "It's fucking awful. I feel like I'm never really going to have a Christmas again." His voice started to pick up speed. "It's not Christmas, you know? But who cares about Christmas? Fuck Christmas! I just miss my sister."

I had started crying the moment he said, *I feel*. I swallowed and cleared my throat, hoping he couldn't hear the tears in my voice. "I'm so sorry."

"Yeah." I heard him sigh.

I wanted to say something, but I had no wisdom to share. Nothing to make it better. The only thing I could give him, he didn't want.

"When are you coming back to town?" he asked.

"January fifth."

"Let's go for a walk when you get back."

I looked down at my feet at the end of the bed. The doctor had given me the okay to remove the walking cast just before exams. I was wearing new snowman socks from my dad. He never knew what to get me, so socks always filled my stocking. He made it out like a clever joke and would say, "Santa filled your stocking with stockings!" A few years ago I began filling his stocking with the same. We'd say "Merry Socksmas!" to one another.

I pointed my red toes. "I'm a little afraid of slipping on the ice. I'm planning on joining the interpretive dance club," I said.

"We'll walk in the mall, then," he said. I couldn't tell if he thought I was being sarcastic about the dance group.

I tried calling him when I got back to campus. At first I accidentally pressed Tara's number in my contacts; she was still listed directly below him. I hung up immediately, my heart racing. I was scared of what would happen next, even though there were only two real possibilities: it would go to voicemail, or I'd hear the automated message indicating the number was no longer in service. Still, I feared some other result, some confrontation I couldn't handle. I considered deleting her number, but it felt too cruel. I lay down on my bed and stared at the ceiling for a while. There was a bug trapped in the plastic dome covering the bulb. It crawled around and fluttered its wings, buzzing against the enclosure. I looked at my phone's contacts again. It was three days before classes would start back up, and the dorm halls were empty. The building felt eerie. I wanted to get out. Frederick didn't answer when I called, and I didn't leave a message. Half an hour later he texted that he was busy the next few days. He suggested we get lunch after his Wednesday class.

But Wednesday arrived, and something "came up." He didn't initiate further plans.

The bathroom in my hall flooded. I overheard in the cafeteria line that a girl had clogged a toilet when she tried to flush a plastic bag full of her vomit.

I walked slowly to the showers a floor above in my flip-flops, a towel and pail of toiletries in arm. Stairs were still difficult. But I didn't mind having to use a new bathroom. There was new unread graffiti in the stalls to keep me occupied from the pain.

> *Della Elkowitz likes it in the ass.*
> *You are beautiful!*
> *Kappa Kappa Gamma bitches for lyfe!*
> *Well-behaved women rarely make history.*
> *Fred Doyle is a whore.*

Reading the last one made me drop my things. It was like seeing your name in the newspaper unexpectedly. It had to have been him. People weren't named Fred anymore. Who had written it? The black markered letters looked faded. As I showered, all I could think about was Frederick's sexual history. I rinsed my hair quickly and later felt the slick of soapy residue at the nape of my neck.

For the first dance practice, eleven girls lined up on the stage of a lecture hall. Linzette, the president of the club, had a round face and a mass of tight curls. She explained that this was not a competitive group.

"If you expect this to be like *Dancing with the Stars*,

you better leave now," she said. She waited a moment. Everyone straightened up and looked around. No one left. "If you're looking for a way to express yourself in a safe space without judgment," she went on, "and you plan to be a positive member of a tight-knit community, I welcome you to stay." Linzette lifted her arms above her head and did a side bend. We followed suit. "I know we have some beginners here, and we have some dancers who have done this for a long time. But I don't want anyone to get intimidated. Just accept where you're at and do what you can with what you've got."

I felt my insides swell with an excitement I hadn't felt since I'd received my college acceptance letter.

"This is about self-expression. It's about creativity." She folded forward and touched her toes. I was careful not to move past a ninety-degree angle. My fingers couldn't even touch my shins. I told myself they might never, at least not this year, and that this was perfectly okay.

We did an exercise where we were asked to have a non-verbal conversation with a partner. My partner twirled around. I swirled my hands around the sides of my head and took slow steps in a circle around her. She jumped, and then lowered her body to the floor, spread her legs into splits. I did a shallow squat and leaned my shoulders to one side, then the other.

I hadn't heard from Frederick in three weeks. I decided to go ahead and call instead of text. It was after a dance practice, so I was feeling particularly optimistic. I wanted a conversation. I wanted that playful banter.

"Did you know you're famous?" I asked as soon as he picked up. After feeling uncomfortable about the bathroom graffiti for the past several weeks, I decided that it was funny. He would find it funny, too.

"You saw my YouTube videos?"

"I mean the tribute to you in the girls' bathroom."

"What?" He sounded alarmed.

"It says, 'Fred Doyle is a whore.'" I laughed.

"Oh, jeeze. Jillian." There was tension in his voice. I didn't expect it. He was the master of laughing things off.

"One of your Johns? Or, I guess *Jills*." I tried to lighten the mood myself.

"We dated a bit. Will you just scrub it off or something?"

"Why do you care?" I scoffed. "You *are* kind of a whore, aren't you?"

"I'm seeing someone. She'll care."

I would have asked more questions if I had waited for the shock to pass. It was stupid to be so surprised, I told myself. Of course he dated girls. Of course he fucked them. I told him I'd leave him alone, and I hung up.

The next day, when I walked out of my statistics class and checked my phone, I found a text from Frederick: "Mall walk?" I didn't respond.

It wasn't until a full month later that we talked. Linzette had emailed the club members the poster image for our upcoming performance. I forwarded the invitation to my parents and a girl I'd met in my creative writing class who seemed interested. Impulsively, I sent it to Frederick. He responded immediately, said he was looking forward to it. I tried to control my excitement. I doubted he'd actually show. I told myself he wasn't worth getting excited for, that replying to his email would make it more upsetting when he flaked. Still, I basked in the flutter of joy that came with seeing his name on the screen.

The performance was on a Thursday night, in the same lecture hall where we practiced. My parents carpooled to the show. My father drove, while my mother texted me updates on his behavior: *He's doing that thing where he sucks his teeth; He refuses to drive the speed limit; Does he get that the other drivers can't hear him when he shouts? I hope we arrive in one piece.*

I did stretches in the hallway. Then I found my purse to check my phone one last time. Nothing from Frederick. Only another text from my mom: *I can only handle being around him so long. Do you think it's okay if I don't sit with him for the show?*

What does it matter to me? I thought. I didn't ask her these kinds of questions. *Sure*, I replied. Linzette called my name and we circled up for one of her pep talks. There were seven of us now. We all wore different outfits, aside from Zeeva and Sara, who were performing a duet to a Sade song and wore matching silver dresses. The rest of us were dancing solo. We'd done our own choreography, according to our own style, artistic history, and physical capabilities. I was in a maroon velvet leotard with gray tights and a black wrap-around skirt. I had a new appreciation for my wardrobe once my casts were gone. I could now take almost any type of clothing on and off without assistance. Linzette asked us to stay focused and not to think about the crowd, only our own bodies. She told us she believed in each of us. She told us she was proud of us, and we couldn't let her down if we tried. Linzette was a sophomore.

My dance was third. As I watched Linzette dance her first piece from the wing, then waited as Ahmad danced his, I wondered if I should have taken that first slot. I would have made everyone else look great by comparison. My right leg, where my tibia had fractured, began to ache. My doctor warned not to put too much weight on it. He'd told me to wait until the following school year to dance. I had practiced going easy on my body, and I eventually worked up to pirouettes. I had always done these on my left foot. But I no longer moved with the same grace I had at twelve: when I was mature enough to understand my body, yet early enough that puberty hadn't ruined my center of gravity. Now I was more unsure than ever. Yet, in some moments, when my spirits were high, being the worst dancer on the team—and knowing it—felt freeing.

Then I was up. I walked onto the center of the stage slowly. I looked over the crowd. I couldn't help myself. My parents were sitting on opposite sides of the first row. Frederick was there. Somewhere in the center of the third or fourth row. I only caught a glimpse of his face long enough to register his name in my mind, short enough to doubt it was really him. My feet found their places: in a V that opened up to the back of the stage. My arms reached towards my right. I tucked my chin to my chest. I pictured Tara's face. The stupid clamor in my head settled.

I'd chosen a track by a Swedish musician whose lyrics I couldn't understand under the synthesizers and beats. I liked its simplicity: voices layered and smoothed by electronic modulation. I swept my arms over my head and felt no pain. I pulled and pushed at the air. I did a pirouette, then a few modest leg swings. I lowered my body to the floor and rolled around. This was the part where the song started building. Pushing myself up was the hardest part. Once I was back on my feet I slid them across the floor as my upper body slumped, my eyes sealed shut. I thought of this move as my zombie moonwalk. Without the interference of vision, my movement felt more and more connected to the music. The beat picked up a bit. I hitched my shoulders up, one then the other. I rolled my head around. I decided I could do the rest of the routine with my eyes closed. Leg swings, slower this time. My arms moved like a ticking clock as the music faded.

Linzette squeezed my shoulder as I left the stage

and passed by her. I took a seat along the carpeted hallway. The ten routines to follow seemed over in a matter of minutes. They passed by me in a thoughtless, timeless calm. I returned to the stage with my fellow dancers and we took our bows.

When the lights over the audience turned back on, my mother rushed the stage to give me a hug. My dad followed soon after, and my mom took a step back. My dad suggested we go to dinner. He said he'd buy me a beer. My mother protested, but I knew she wouldn't stop him. I looked around for Frederick, but I couldn't find him.

"Are you Whimsy?" A redhead with cat-eye glasses approached me. My first thought was that this was his girlfriend. I said yes.

"This guy sitting next to me asked me to give this to you." She handed me a potted plant, a purple hyacinth. As soon as I had the cellophane-wrapped pot in both hands, she was gone.

There was a small decorative stake in the soil. On one side were the care directions. On the other side, he had written a message in careful cursive: *Congrats, Zee! I like your moves.*

Nobody wrote in cursive anymore.

What You
Do Is

Wednesdays I had lunch duty at school, which meant I spent thirty minutes leaning against a wall. I gnawed on a protein bar. Ken, the algebra teacher, had Wednesdays too. It embarrassed me to watch Ken make his rounds, circling tables, interjecting himself into the students' conversations. I wanted to shake him. But occasionally a student was receptive to his joke and then I would find myself feeling jealous.

The warning bell rang. Ken walked with a group of sixth graders. They spread across the whole width of the wall, talking excitedly about quiz bowl. I was stuck behind them, shuffling slowly. Once we reached the fork in the hallway, Ken gave each of them a high five. I squeezed by him as his hand hung in the air waiting for the final kid's palm. I unlocked my classroom door and heard the slap.

"See you dudes later," Ken said as he departed.

In class, I extended my students' independent reading time for the afternoon while I composed an email to Judith, outlining our female students' needs for body-positive self-expression. Admittedly, I wasn't great at waiting to think over ideas I was excited about. I wanted to take action right away. I finally felt there was something I could do well at this school.

As class was wrapping up, I asked the students, "Who here is interested in dance?"

"Like a Christmas dance?"

"Not dance the noun," I explained. "Dance the *verb*. Like *performance*."

The girls looked around the room to see if any of their friends had raised their hands. Not one. I looked at Cynthia in the front row; she was hyperactive and gave inadvertent dance performances while seated at her desk on a daily basis. She shrugged at me.

The kids headed to their final period, a study hall. My group of students, mostly from my first period class, trickled in. I turned off one of the sets of overhead fluorescents. I've learned that this calms the students, that they work more quietly in this lowered lighting. While they finished math problems, drew molecules, and read their copies of *Walk Two Moons*, I did research.

At the end of the day, Judith popped her head into my classroom. "I got your email." She gave me a thumbs up. "Stop by my office tomorrow morning."

She continued down the hall, and I grinned. Maybe this would redeem me from that lunchbox-throwing incident. *Coach Quinn*, my brain recited.

I stopped at a Tim Horton's on the way to school the next morning to pick up a muffin for Judith. When I arrived, she was in her office with a parent. I sat in front of the secretary's desk. The parent left Judith's office, his arms wrapped tightly around a folder and his face horror-stricken.

I stood in the doorway. Judith was writing something down on a sticky note. Her halo of bleached ringlets vibrated as she scribbled furiously. I placed the muffin next to her keyboard.

"It's blueberry."

"Thank you, hun." She set down her pen and stood from her chair. "Let's talk in the copy room."

I followed her past the supply closet, where she picked up a ream of goldenrod colored paper. I told her about my history with dance, my experiences on the dance team during my first year at college—how it got me out of my shell and boosted my confidence during a difficult year.

As I spoke, she made sympathetic noises: "Mmm," "Oh," "Right, right," "Absolutely." It was encouraging. Once we made it to the copier she opened the drawer and swapped out the white paper with the goldenrod, added a flier for parent-teacher conferences to the scanner, and plugged a command into the keypad.

"A dance club could be really transformative for a lot of these girls," I said, one hand resting on the mailboxes. Once I discovered my habit of overly gesticulating when nervous, I'd developed a coping mechanism of clutching or leaning on any piece of furniture nearby.

"What time of year would the season be? You can't poach students from cheer or tumbling. Victoria would kill you," she chuckled, though I knew she was serious. Victoria—with her deep, commanding voice, always throwing around the word "data" during staff meetings—scared me.

"I don't think this would attract the same kind of student. And it's not competitive. We could start and end the season, so to speak, whenever."

"I wouldn't be so sure, Whimsy. Those cheer girls belong to Antoinette's," she said, meaning the dance school down the street.

I explained that this was different: modern dance, I said, with strong emphasis.

Judith cocked her head to the side, the sound of the copier whooshing behind her.

"Interpretive—er—improvisational dance. It's more theatrical. Not necessarily choreographed."

She narrowed her eyes. "Are we talking weird, hippie stuff? Like Kate Bush?"

I assured Judith the performances wouldn't be too bizarre for parents, that we'd save the improv for closed practices. She printed out the paperwork: a spreadsheet outlining payment methods for facilitating non-sport activities—I'd receive fifty cents per student per hour during extracurricular club meetings outside of my contractual teaching time—and a copy of the cheer team's injury liability waiver.

"Use this as a template, and make your own sheet for try-outs."

"I was planning on accepting everyone," I said. "I

don't want this to be exclusionary."

She told me that I'd be smart to only let the students who would "favorably represent our school" onto the team. As I walked back to my classroom, my stomach turned and sank the way it did mornings after I'd gotten too little sleep. I didn't like the idea of auditions. But it occurred to me that if Judith really cared so much about how our school looked, I could always edit the list of dancers before any public performances.

During lunch that day, Stephanya brought her tray of nachos into my classroom. I had invited her to my room for extra help on an essay last month. She'd begun coming into my class for lunch nearly every day since, at first under the guise of needing tutoring. Then she asked if she could show me a poem. Then more poems, and every week. Stephanya had a harelip and spoke so quietly I could barely hear her. While her awkwardness was painful to be around and her presence was, at times, irritating, I tried to seem happy to see her each time she came to my class—even when I was swamped and had no time or patience for chit chat.

"Hey, Stephanya!" I said. My enthusiasm startled her. She had been sitting silently, picking strands of limp lettuce off of her chips for the past several minutes.

"Yeah?" she said quietly, gazing up from her still-downcast head.

"I'm starting a modern dance club, and I really think you should join." It would be a good opportunity for her to make friends. She wouldn't have to talk much, and she'd be lumped together with her fellow artistic weirdos.

"Uh…" she dunked a bean-limp chip into plasticky cheese dip.

"It's not like the kind of dance teams you're familiar with. It's really about expressing yourself with your body. No rules."

She was chewing her nachos, looking at me inquisitively. She had recently dyed her hair. Last week it was fire engine red, but it had already faded. Now it resembled the hue of Flamin' Hot Cheetos with most of the red, spicy dust brushed off. I found these, half-crushed and strewn about the hallways, on a regular basis.

She sipped from her chocolate milk, then pushed her mouth to one side of her face. I waited for her reply. This might be a real turning point for her, I decided. She had to join.

"It'll make you feel free," I said.

Stephanya helped me post fliers throughout the school. I wrote a script about the club for the secretary to read over morning announcements during the two weeks leading up to auditions. I reminded my students about the team every other day. Still, they said they weren't interested. Not even Stephanya raised her hand when I asked her class who was planning to audition. I figured at least one or two students in each class would show up. They just didn't want to draw attention to themselves in front of their peers.

Since basketball practice was taking place in the gym, the try-outs were held in the cafeteria. I found music for the individual portion: a Navajo flute track mixed with electro-pop beats. I would see each student dance to thirty seconds of the music. Afterwards, I would observe their teamwork skills as they choreographed a short group routine.

Three students showed up. I led them in warm-up stretches. It had only been fifteen minutes since final period released; I hoped some students were just running late, busy changing into gym clothes. My vision kept ping-ponging between the clock and the door. Two more girls, wearing tight leggings and athletic tank tops, approached the doorway to the cafeteria and stopped before entering. One pulled out a cell phone and showed the other. They gasped, then giggled. I didn't recognize them. They must have been eighth graders.

"Are you girls here for dance?" I asked from across the room, the suspense unbearable. I sat on the cold tiled floor and set my feet straight in front of me. The trio of dancers did the same.

The girls in the doorway didn't answer me. I would have scolded them for being late, told them to step inside quickly or scram, but I didn't want to scare them off. Eventually, they came inside—still without acknowledging me—and set their backpacks beneath a folded up lunch table.

"Come join us. We're just warming up." I folded forward and instructed everyone to reach for their toes. If they couldn't reach their toes, shins were fine. If they couldn't reach their shins, knees were just as well. I told them that everyone's body is different and to honor where they were at. The two newcomers looked at each other and smirked. They folded forward, just the same.

"Now, we're going to do an improv activity to introduce you to modern dance." I stood up, and gestured for everyone to stand and form a circle. "This activity is meant for you to express yourself using your body in a completely original way. Show us who you are with your movements. Since I see some unfamiliar faces, I'd like you to first share your name, grade, and something about yourself—maybe tell us a bit about why you're here."

A scrawny kid, the only boy, began. He wasn't one of my students, but I recognized him as a member of a large Filipino family in the district. I had at least one of his cousins or siblings in each of my classes. "Um, I'm Alvin Santos, sixth grade. I do tap at Antoinette's, but my mom said I have to get involved with a school activity this year, and my sister told me about this club." He shrugged and looked down at the floor. I started the music. He wore soft shoes and began a series of tap movements. He stared at his feet as he shuffled and stepped.

I paused the music. "Now, Alvin, I want you to move out of your comfort zone. Try and forget what you know from tap. Take all the steps you've learned, erase them from your head, and just move the way your spirit tells you." I felt a jolt of anxiety upon recognizing my mistake in using the word "spirit." I hoped I wouldn't get any phone calls from parents who thought I was leading some cultish, religious activity.

I started the music again. Alvin stood still for a few seconds, like he was wracking his brain to think of what to do. He put his arms in the air and waved them back and forth, as though he were listening to a hair band ballad. I waited to see what he would do next. He began turning as he waved his arms. Then his feet returned to tapping.

"No, no, no," I said, frustrated. I paused the music again.

He stopped. "I'm sorry." He looked scared.

I sighed. "It's okay, Alvin. I know it's habit. We're just going to have to work a little harder to help you quit following your habits and start listening to your heart."

I put my hands on my hips and turned to the next student, one of the latecomers, who introduced herself as Gia. She moved within the half-circle our bodies had formed. I started the music again. She pulled her fists up at her armpits and began punching the air in front of her while shaking her butt.

"Twerk it, girl!" her friend said, laughing.

The other kids started giggling.

For a moment I shuddered, as I do every time I hear laughter directed at a child. I was ready to yell at the giggling girl, maybe even throw her out. Then a huge grin spread over Gia's face, and I knew she was in on the joke, loving the attention. My face grew hot.

"Try some other moves now, Gia. Something more original." I snapped twice for some reason.

She spread her knees and dropped her bottom to the floor. She rolled up slowly. Her friend cheered her on. Gia and I made eye contact. My face must have revealed my anger, because she quickly shifted her tactic. She shot her arms at her sides and swooped around like an airplane. I was ready to pounce and strangle her. Before I could intervene (in a more lawful manner), she did a grande jeté and followed it up with a series of beautiful movements. Once the thirty seconds were up, I paused the music. The students all clapped. Even I clapped.

I asked Stephanya to go next. She didn't move. I repeated my request, and her eyes glazed over in terror. I walked to her, lightly touched my hand to her forearm. "It's just like making a poem with your body. You've got this." I said.

Her movements were self-conscious, much more restrained than Gia's. But about ten seconds into her music, she began to ease into herself. The way she shut her eyes for a few seconds at a time, the way her face seemed more relaxed than usual—I could tell dance was working on her.

Next up was Gia's friend, Torrey, then Maureen. After Gia took it seriously, it seemed to give the other students permission to take it seriously too. I felt pleased, relieved.

I told everyone they did a great job and announced that next I would give them thirty minutes to choreograph a one-minute song together. I played the music for them, a song by Enya.

"We want to do the Lady Gaga dance from the 'Bad Romance' video," Gia said. Her sidekick, Torrey, echoed beside her with a nasally, "Yeah!"

"If you do someone else's choreography, that's no longer improvisation, right?"

"But we all want to do it," Torrey whined.

"Well—"

"Who here wants to do Lady Gaga?" Gia raised her hand, quickly followed by Torrey. Alvin and Maureen raised their hands, shyly below their shoulders. Finally, Stephanya slid her hand up. I glared at her and scoffed.

Soon after the Gaga coups, I heard the squeaky rolling wheels of the janitor's bucket. He began mopping the cafeteria, oblivious to the people or activities around him. "We're still working in here, Bill," I called to him. But he couldn't hear me over the Sinatra blaring through his ear buds. I took this as a sign and told the students we would meet again the next week.

"Am I in?" Maureen asked.

"Yeah," I pursed my lips. "You're all in." I held my

hand out to Stephanya and she gave me a high five. I went around the circle and high-fived each student. Torrey rolled her eyes as she raised her hand. I still felt queasy, ill at ease, but a sliver of my initial hope for the team remained intact.

When I got home, it was still early, and I was all caught up on grading and planning. That hadn't happened before. I sat on my couch, frozen with indecision. I could take a bath and try to get to bed early, catch up on sleep. The apartment felt so small, and I still had energy. I texted Miri to ask if she wanted to get a drink.

Can't. Next week?

I looked through my contact list. I'd pause on one name, then realize I hadn't spoken to them since high school. It would be too much of a production to meet up with an old friend and have to talk them through my life since they'd last seen me. There weren't too many holes to fill in; anyone I'd known that long could see pictures of what I looked like now. But people still insist on talking through it all, pretending they don't know what you share online of your day-to-day life.

Ken had invited me to a brewery with some other teachers the first few Fridays of the school year. But after I declined several times, he stopped asking. From the way the other teachers talked about their weekends on Mondays I was certain they hung out with one another, and I had been missing out. I logged onto my school email account and found his number from the contacts list. I didn't want to sound too weird about texting him to get a drink, despite the rush of excitement, so I added: *I'm bored and somehow don't have grading to do!*

He responded quickly, saying he was about to make himself a sandwich, but that we could get a bite at Applebee's instead.

I like to face the wall at restaurants whenever possible. The waiter warned me that happy hour would be ending in five minutes as he sat me at a corner booth and suggested I try the blue raspberry margarita. I didn't have the brain space to think about what I wanted to drink, so I said sure. I was beginning to worry Ken might mistake this for a date. But I figured if I kept the conversation on school, he would be clear about the nature of our meeting. I'd put on lipstick before leaving the house; I rubbed it off on the back on my hand. I buttoned my shirt up to the collar. Shortly after the margarita arrived, so did Ken.

"Hey, kiddo," he said, sliding into the booth and removing his coat.

I looked behind me for a student, maybe a child he might have dragged along. But he was talking to me. "Oh, hi. How are you?"

"Decent, yeah. Already pounding the blue stuff? You hanging in there?"

I pulled the drink away from my lips. It was my first sip. "Yeah, I'm fine." I straightened my posture, pushed the glass away.

"Everybody's first year of teaching is rough." Ken looked at me with pity. He pressed his lips together tightly, so his mustache covered his bottom lip.

"Hmm?" I was caught off-guard.

"It seemed like you might be having a tough time of it, is all I mean. I figured you were looking for a pep talk." He shook his head, noticing my defensiveness. Ken was perceptive for a math teacher. It irritated me thoroughly.

"I'm really doing okay. I'm starting a dance club. I'm not, like, drowning here."

"My apologies." He knocked the table with his fist.

The waiter set down two ice waters. Ken wrapped his hands around his and thanked the waiter. He ordered a root beer and a grilled chicken wrap.

"Watching my cholesterol," he said, turning back to me. "Old man stuff." He smiled.

I ordered mozzarella sticks. And then I shut down. Just leaned back in my seat and let Ken carry the conversation. He told me about his kids, two girls, eight and six, who he had on the weekends. I smiled. I nodded. I took sips of the margarita until it was gone, and I ate every last mozzarella stick, even when I ran out of dipping sauce and room in my stomach. I washed it down with water. Ken asked me if I wanted children.

"I don't know," I said. I felt I couldn't elaborate any further than that.

Ken insisted on paying, saying, "I rememb.
student loans." I had promised myself not to let
him pay when I'd sat down at the booth. Now I just
thanked him.

He stood up after quickly figuring the tip and
signing the receipt. Ken put on his jacket. "Are you
staying?" he asked when I didn't move to gather my
belongings or put on my coat.

I shrugged. He said goodnight and left. I felt
lonelier than before.

Adult
Coloring

At mom's place, the card table was covered with pages of her girlfriend's soon-to-be-self-published adult coloring book. It's a small one bedroom, the edges of the table just a couple feet from the couch on one end, the television on the other. I was still getting used to calling it her apartment, and not "Barb's apartment." It was a government-subsidized building for people with disabilities. For a while, I thought it was supposed to be a secret that my mom had become a full-time resident and no longer just a houseguest.

"What's in there?" My mother pointed to my rolling suitcase.

"My stuff." I yanked it over the molding along the floor at the doorway. It made a loud clunk.

"You're staying one night, Whimsy. I have everything you need here." She was offended any time my needs exceeded or differed from her own.

"Where's Barb?"

"She's taking our neighbor's dogs for a walk. You remember Greg, right? The handicapped guy? He's got two terriers."

"Oh," I said, though this description hadn't narrowed it down. "I don't think they like the term handicapped." I sat down on a stool at the counter in the kitchen. They didn't have a dining room. The counter and the couch were usually the only places to sit.

"Barb says *handicapped*."

I didn't push further. During my sporadic visits, I sensed an unspoken divide between the residents with physical disabilities and the residents with mental ones. Or maybe I just assumed it. The neighbors who had been over—their friends from the building, presumably—hadn't had physically noticeable differences.

My mother poured us each a glass of iced tea. More like cold tea, though; she didn't keep ice in the house. She didn't believe in it due to an article she'd read decades ago in *Reader's Digest*.

"C'mon," she said and carried the glasses of cold tea to the card table. I followed, then struggled to pull the chair out far enough to sit comfortably. The edge of the table pushed against my ribs. "Barb wants us to color in some of these pages, so she can feature them on the cover."

Barb had been working on the book for months. My mother updated me on her progress during our phone calls. "She's got twenty three drawings now," and, "She just has to finish her section on flowering fruit trees." It was made up of illustrations of Michigan's native flowers. They had dreams of selling the books to schools. My mother asked that I promise to bring it up with my principal. I said maybe.

I grabbed the colored pencils and a photocopy of an apple blossom. My mom was already filling in the petals of a trillium with bright blue crayon.

"Mom, I think that flower is supposed to be white."

"A trillium?"

I nodded hesitantly, ready for her to go on another tangent about how Kinko's was robbing them blind.

"You sure? I thought it was blue."

"You're thinking of a bellflower, or maybe an aster."

"Oh, well, doesn't it look gorgeous like this?" She held it up to me. "I don't think it matters. I'm using my creativity." She continued coloring. She looked happy. I'd never seen my mother so at ease before she'd started seeing Barb. She was never one for creativity, and generally a pessimist. A *realist*, she'd say. I thought of her response when I told her I wanted to study dance—hysterical. And her reaction had worked: I switched my major to education and decided to become a teacher, like she'd been.

Mom grunted as she lifted herself out of her seat and turned on the CD player. Carole King's "I Feel the Earth Move" began. She returned to her seat and bobbed her head side to side. I wondered what it would have been like if I were raised by this woman.

"I can't believe you're so into this," I said. My tone sounded snottier than I'd intended.

"What?" She looked up. "Coloring?"

I snorted and nodded.

"I'm into it because Barb is. Sometimes you need

to try out your partner's interests to connect with them." She returned to her coloring with new focus. She stilled her head, brought her face closer to the paper while she carefully outlined the edges of the flower. "You're gonna have to send me a clipping of your article."

"It's on the Free Press website," I said. They only printed the paper once a week now. The pages were reserved for real news.

"Okay, then print out a copy for me," she said.

I said I would, but I wasn't sure. I thought I might wait and see if she forgot about it altogether. If I didn't call attention to it, I knew no one would read it. People my age didn't read the Free Press. My students certainly didn't either. In the days after the piece appeared on the website, I anticipated my coworkers mentioning it to me. I avoided the copy room during high-traffic times. But no one said a thing. If I wanted anyone to read it, I'd have to share it on social media, push it in the faces of the people I knew and vaguely knew. But I didn't do that. Instead I felt too vulnerable. Rikesh's words made me feel seen.

Without looking up from her drawing, my mother asked what she really wanted to know about. "And that journalist? Have you talked to him at all?"

"I've seen him a couple times."

She smiled, and then returned to her coloring. "You took my advice, then."

"Not exactly. He called me again before I got the

chance to call him back," I lied.

My mom said that was even better.

After the first couple dates with Rikesh, I had convinced myself that I didn't have time for a relationship, that we weren't compatible anyway. I had to focus on school, and myself. I had resisted picking up or returning his calls. He gave up. I kept thinking about him. Finally, I called late one night after going through half a bottle of wine. Now that I had given up, I was able to relax and speak to him like a normal human being. We had a two-hour conversation. He asked me to come over. I said no, still unconvinced it was worth the emotional risk. I told my mother this. She nodded along, said, "Right, right" repeatedly, as though she'd heard this story before. This was her way of saying she knew me so well that she could predict what I was going to do in every situation, and so my explanation was unnecessary.

When Barb came home, my mother attempted to make quesadillas while Barb and I cleaned up the pages and supplies. Barb slipped each sheet of paper into its own plastic sleeve in a large binder. She complimented me on my coloring work. Then I set the card table for dinner. I watched Barb touch my mother's back so gently as she squeezed behind her, reaching for the hot sauce in the upper cabinet.

People with gay children often say they "knew all along." But I wasn't sure how it usually worked with parents. It had never occurred to me my mother might be attracted to women. To children, parents are either together or apart, happy or unhappy. Not gay or straight. I can see it in hindsight, though. Now that I'd gotten used to the idea, and Barb, herself, I liked them together. Barb was the one with the diagnosis, but my mother wasn't the most stable, either. Banded together, they got by, and I could worry less.

That night, I lay on the air mattress in the space where the table had been. I was facing the apartment entrance. A light shined through the bottom of the door from the hallway. Shadows interrupted the stream of light when people walked by. Over the course of the next hour, I heard the slow aluminum clomp of walkers, the electric hum of motorized wheelchairs, several pairs of feet shuffling by. I grew tired of wondering about all the people, so I grabbed my pillow and flopped my body around in the opposite direction. Now I was facing the sliding doors that led to the balcony. The vertical blinds were drawn, but the slits were still illuminated by the street lights in the parking lot. I groaned and reached for my phone, which was plugged into the wall and lay on the floor. I re-read Rikesh's last text. He'd asked me how my week at school had been. I hadn't replied. It wasn't that I wanted him to feel rejected. But I didn't want to seem too eager. And I was trying to think of a clever response. In the past, I'd wasted opportunities to have the upper hand.

Are you awake? I wrote, then set down the phone,

rolled away from the wall, and pulled the cover over my head. He wasn't going to reply. It was one in the morning. Then I heard a vibration against the carpet. I rolled back over and picked up the phone.

Yeah. Are you partying? Or do you have insomnia?

A little bit of both, I said.

Take a shot of rum to help with the former, a shot of warm milk for the latter.

I made a dumb joke about mixing the two together to make a new cocktail. A "dark and milky." Then, impulsively, I suggested I come over and he make me one.

I folded up the blankets, wrote Mom and Barb a note on the back of a scrap coloring book copy, and lifted my suitcase over the ridge in the doorway, so it wouldn't catch and make a noise.

It was almost a two-hour drive. I'd only seen the outside of his place, when I picked him up for glow bowling the last time I'd seen him. That was my idea of a date. I regretted it immediately upon arriving at the bowling alley. I hadn't bowled since I was in middle school. I quickly realized I hated everything about it. Rikesh had feigned enthusiasm, cheering for me, gently taunting me. We were both terrible, and it was just depressing—until we tried placing the ball at the end of the lane, then pushing with both hands. We concocted a new game where we competed for whose ball took the longest to reach the end of the lane. We timed each other using his stopwatch. I remembered pointing out all the lint on his sweater, which glowed neon blue under the black light. Rather than laughing along with me, he set his ball down and spent the next several minutes picking off the lint. I hadn't expected that at all. He'd seemed so at ease in his body, as though nothing about his physical nature could bother him.

I turned the radio to a hip-hop station. I needed a beat to keep me alert for the drive. My mind was wide-awake, but my eyelids were starting to droop.

When I pulled up to his duplex, I began to feel anxious. I parked on the street. His place was one of those houses where, at first glance, it appears to be a typical single family home, but then you notice there are two identical front doors, side by side. It took me a moment to remember which was his. Then I noticed the striped curtains: black and white, like something out of the movie *Beetlejuice*, which I'd thought about when I'd picked him up. The unit beside his had bland windows, with regular plastic blinds. I saw the curtains move, his head poke out from behind them.

Rikesh opened the door as I stepped onto the concrete porch. He said nothing, just smiled, then turned away and walked towards the kitchen. I shut the door behind me and followed him. On the counter, there were two steaming mugs.

I stood in the hallway between the kitchen and the living room. He grabbed the mugs and slid past me. He set them down on the coffee table and sat on the couch.

"Come here," he said, softly.

I joined him on the couch. I watched him sip from his mug. With the room's only light coming from the lamp behind him, I could see the steam wash over his face. I lifted my drink, tasted the delicate flavors of chamomile and honey, followed by the hot sting of whiskey at the back of my throat.

"Hot toddy," he said. "I'm out of milk."

His tone and the ease on his face calmed my anxiety. It was like he was telling me I no longer had to put on a show: to force myself to be chatty and festive and likable, the way I'd felt in the bowling alley. *We might get to just be quiet together*, I thought.

"What did you do at your mom's?"

I had texted that I was at her place before driving over, reassuring him that she would understand if I left. Rikesh asked me what she was like, if we got along. I told him about how we'd grown much closer since I'd moved out. How she was easier to get along with now that she was happy. He laughed at my impressions of her. He made empathetic noises, little grunts and hmms when I described my guilt. I felt I should have been a better daughter when she was grieving her divorce.

"You were grieving too, though."

I took a sip of my tea and licked the traces of liquid from my lips. He watched me. He wasn't afraid to, like so many others.

Later, I would feel this exchange had been

planned for weeks. He was completely aware of his intent behind every empathetic noise. I was aware of the intent behind sharing my incredibly ordinary mother-inflicted wounds. But maybe this is all rationale. Perhaps I still haven't learned that a person who is kind is also capable of doing great harm. For this evening, though, the lamplight did not reveal metacognition. We were in a half-awake state. We were our hot toddies and the throw pillows our bodies gradually eased into.

We drank our tea for a while in silence, our eyes fixated on the opposite side of the room, where the TV stood in the center of the picture window. In my peripheral vision, I saw him finally move. He turned towards me. I turned and we looked at each other. His expression was serious, one of longing. But my nervous response was a goofy smile. I had zero ability to remain cool in this situation. Usually my nervous grin elicited one on his face. But he simply moved closer. I set my mug down. Then my head was in his hands. Not forcefully, but not too hesitantly, either. I liked the pressure of his palms cupping the back of my head, like he felt some ownership. Yet he seemed to lack the greed which often accompanies the fear that ownership will be taken away. He kissed me differently, too, almost conversationally. I pulled my leg over his lap, straddling him. I hadn't looked down on him before. At this angle, I noticed the length of his eyelashes. So long and black. I told him so. He closed his eyes in a slow motion blink. He kissed my neck and asked me to go to the bedroom. I wouldn't let him undress me. But soon I did it myself.

I get the feeling you can smell if someone's a good person. The scents of so many men, even just passing by in a public space, have made me gag, but I don't mean the scent of sweat or filth. I mean a natural odor that smells *not right*, an instinctual warning sign. I felt like I couldn't get enough of Rikesh in my nostrils. I breathed so deeply. At a point, my face brushed against his scalp and I thought, *This must be the kind of breathing my therapist was trying to teach me*.

After I went to the bathroom, I was surprised to find him sitting on the bed, still naked, staring at me. It was like he'd been watching the door, waiting for me to return.

Instead of joining him, I approached the floating wooden shelves, lined with fossils, geodes, and colorful polished rocks. It looked like a precocious fourth grader's collection—if that fourth grader had continued to add to his collection for the next twenty years.

I picked a polished golden-colored stone up and rubbed it between my fingers. "Tiger's eye?"

Rikesh came closer, pushed the hair away from my face. "Yes," he said and kissed my cheek—the scarred side. For once, I didn't pull away. I didn't even flinch.

"My face doesn't gross you out?" I asked, without taking my eyes off the stones.

"Of course not." He rested his chin on my shoulder and picked up another stone, a purple one. "Do you know this one?"

"Amethyst?"

"It's my birthstone."

"I think I might be opal."

He picked up a small yellow stone. "Don't have any opal, but you can keep this one." Rikesh placed it in my hand.

It was all too much generosity for me. I put the citrine back on the shelf, but thanked him still.

I thought of asking him more questions about rocks, showing some interest. But I was far too tired. I crawled into bed, and he followed. He pulled the covers up and brushed his hand over the comforter, smoothing the fabric over my thighs.

When I was born, my mother said, I was a serious baby. My eyebrows were set in a permanent crumple, my face a scowl. My father joked that they should name me "Happy." My mother immediately vetoed the idea, on account of the horrible son named Happy in *Death of a Salesman*. But she went with my father's line of thinking and considered a new list of names that exuded light-heartedness. Suddenly my originally planned name, Joanna, my maternal great-grandmother's, no longer suited me. They watched me gurgle, grunt, and furrow my brows as they shot off names: Joy? Hope? Song? Laughter? Glitter? Pansy?

Skills

Miri told me this was a skill that could be learned.

She said, "You have to practice having sex without emotions."

We'd been discussing a reality show about swingers.

I didn't believe her.

Miri said she didn't need to worry about this anymore—her way of changing the topic back to William, their upcoming nuptials. I'd brought up the show as a way to steer the conversation towards Rikesh.

I was dying to tell someone about him. It was the reason I'd called her to get together in the first place. I wanted to discuss the details. I wanted her to ask me questions and care about my answers. I wanted her excitement to reflect upon and reinforce my own.

But now that I was here, looking at the photos of flower arrangements on the screen of her phone, I reevaluated my expectations. Those moments with Rikesh were a delicate object I held in my hand. Every time I opened my fingers to reveal it, I'd risk manipulating the memory.

I usually went to his place. I'm not sure why, but that first week after we slept together we got into a sort of routine. He cooked us dinner, while I sat at the table, exhausted from a day of teaching. I liked to watch him move. So unselfconscious. He was tall, large of frame, but appeared lighter than you'd expect. He tended to lift off his heels. I noticed his socks raise from the faux wood flooring in his kitchen and it reminded me of my ballet classmates growing up. You could tell who was truly dedicated to dance based upon how they set their feet when they were walking through the locker room or waiting for their mothers outside the studio. When they weren't trying to dance at all.

That Saturday, I told Rikesh I wanted him in my apartment; I would make him dinner this time. He brought over a loaf of homemade bread. "You just couldn't help yourself, could you?" I said. It would have been annoying if anyone else had done it. But that was his nature, constantly proffering gifts.

I don't know why I chose Borscht. I'd never made it before. Something about the color that was so alluring, impressive, rich. I ordered Rikesh to sit on the couch in the living room area. It was a studio apartment, so we were never far from one another. After a few minutes of reading *Freak the Mighty*, the book I'd been reading with my seventh graders, he got up and opened my fridge. I liked having someone around to invade my space, examine my things. It happened so rarely. He retrieved the contents of the fruit drawer: a Granny Smith apple and an orange whose best days were behind it. He found a cutting board and a knife, and he began cutting the fruit into tooth-sized chunks. I looked over at him from the pot where I was browning onions. Rikesh had that signature smirk as he pulled two glasses down from the cabinet. His neutral state was joy. He tossed the fruit into the glasses and added a few glugs of the three-dollar red wine from my counter—impromptu sangria.

We were hungry. We each ate a slice of his bread. We drank the sangria, which mostly just tasted like wine. Rikesh told me not to drink it all, to let the second half steep in the fruit. We set our glasses on the table. He stirred the pot, lowered the flame, propped the lid on partially, and grabbed my hand. He led me to the bed, which was covered with laundry I hadn't yet folded.

"You're beautiful," he said.

"No, I'm not."

"Yes, you are."

"What's beautiful about me?" It felt clichéd. But this was my chance to ask, to hear someone tell me how they saw me, to find out how differently someone else's eyes worked under the direction of another brain.

"Can't you just let me say what I want to say? Why do you always have to push for more?"

I apologized. His face softened again, and he kissed me.

Later, when we tried the soup, the beets were still crunchy. We let our bowls go cold on the table and filled up on bread instead.

• • •

Our drinks came, and Miri and I traded sips. She ordered a Cosmopolitan. I got a dirty martini, clouded with olive brine. While I drank, I still felt that discontented itch on the top layer of my skin. I still felt sad, not being able to tell her my good news. I nodded along and answered her when she asked my opinion on her decision to do a cookie bar instead of a chocolate fountain. She fished an olive out of my drink with a fork and ate it. Once she'd run out of new wedding developments to share, she told me about a TV show I should be watching. She went through a roster of new shows I hadn't heard of: "We love _____," and "We think _____ is overrated," and "We didn't used to like_____, but it's gotten better this season." I wondered if she and William ever disagreed about anything.

It must have been the smugness of her repeating the word *we*. I cracked.

"Guess who's been getting laid?" I rubbed the tip of my finger along the rim of my glass. It didn't sound like me at all. It came out like a Matthew McConaughey impression.

"*What!* How come you didn't tell me? Who is it?"

A little thrill in me twittered as she leaned closer.

"Do you remember that story about me on the Free Press website?"

She nodded and slurped her drink.

"That journalist."

She squealed and asked who made the first move, how it all went down. It was amazing how much I relished the attention of someone whose company I no longer enjoyed. But something about her reaction was addictive. I remembered every hand job she ever reported to me in high school, when the only romantic encounters I had were online conversations unworthy of gossip. Now I was the one with the story.

We'd slept together five times in the past two weeks. I hadn't been getting enough sleep. But at school I wasn't fatigued. Miri asked me what he was like in bed. I began to describe the way he touched me. Having little to compare it to, I couldn't make sweeping judgments, only share the hard evidence. This is when the twittering feeling in my chest sputtered and sank. These moments were no longer all mine. She asked when I would see him next, and I told her tomorrow. I changed the subject before she could ask another question. I brought up the guest list. She asked me if I would bring Rikesh as my wedding date. I laughed awkwardly in response and shrugged. I finished the dregs of my cocktail and marveled over how I could stand to know myself well enough to anticipate my reaction in any given social situation, yet still act against my best interests. Was it impulse or self-sabotage? Impulsive self-sabotage?

Miri got a text from William and said she had to go. She started to ask the waiter for two bills, but I interrupted and asked for just the one. It made me feel a little better, to take control over this one thing.

The next morning I picked up Rikesh to drive him to the train station. He was going to Chicago for a conference, to present a paper on optical mineralogy. I liked the term optical mineralogy; I repeated it in my head like a poem long after I'd forgotten what it meant. Rikesh was quiet in the car. I asked him why, and he said he was nervous about his presentation. He'd packed more than I thought would be necessary for a four-day trip. His duffel bag filled up my back seat, and his garment bag lay across it. I reassured him that he was a natural orator.   He asked how I knew.

"I'm an English teacher," I told him. "I know these things."

I pulled into the station parking lot. He started to gather his things to get out of the car, but I suggested he just wait here with me until the train arrived. I cracked the windows and turned off the car. I heard no train approaching, just the usual whooshing of cars that I'd learned to ignore. The station was next to a pizza parlor, and the scent of garlic wafted over. I wondered aloud, half-joking, about who was ordering pizzas at ten in the morning.

"They're probably just doing prep work. Making sauce and dough, you know?"

"You're so literal," I said and leaned over to kiss him. It was a long enough kiss that I could inhale and exhale a few times. The warm air from his nostrils tickled my face.

We pulled away at the train's whistle, followed by

the rumbling of the tracks.

He placed his hands at the sides of my face, covering my ears.

I watched him leave the car, jogging towards the train with his duffel on one arm, his suit jackets draped over the other.

While Rikesh was away at the conference, I vowed to give him space, set some boundaries. My therapist said boundaries weren't my strong suit. I would only text him once a day. I was allowed to respond to his texts, but I could only initiate the conversation once, and I could only respond to his texts at a one-to-one ratio. I didn't think normal people had to put these parameters on themselves, but I knew what would happen if I didn't. I'd been putting off asking him to Miri's wedding. I kept telling myself I needed more time to gauge if we had that kind of relationship. But the wedding was next weekend, and I was cutting it close. I had to waste one day's text on asking him. I proposed the plan the first night he was gone. "Sounds fun," he responded. And that was it for night one's text conversation. It was minimal like that for all four days he was gone. The weekdays weren't as difficult. I focused on staying on top of my grading and lesson plans. I searched the library for modern dance DVDs to show the girls at practice. In the evenings, I slipped into a wine-and-reality-television-induced sleep on the couch.

I was a little hurt that Miri hadn't asked me to be a

bridesmaid. Not that I wanted to stand up there during the ceremony, asking to be stared at and compared to the other bridesmaids by the guests. I wondered if Miri thought I wasn't pretty enough, if my scars would ruin her photos. She was superficial like that. Even though we didn't see each other regularly these days, I still thought of her as one of my closest friends. I realized she was the closest thing I had to a best friend besides my mom.

I offered to drive Rikesh and I the forty-mile route to the wedding. The invitation said it was a barn reception. The return envelope was wrapped in a twine bow. I wore cowboy boots and a plaid dress.

"Well yeehaw, I say," Rikesh slid into the passenger seat, wearing a navy pinstripe suit. I should have told him, I thought. Our patterns clashed entirely.

Rikesh agreed to be the navigator—in other words, repeat the directions given by my phone's GPS. I put on our pop station. I began to sing along to a song about slutty girls who were looking only for money. I turned to Rikesh. He was staring at his phone.

"Do you know this song?" I asked.

"Hmm?" After a moment, he looked up.

I repeated myself.

"Oh, I don't." He typed into his phone.

I felt anxious, not knowing who he was talking to.

"I'm sorry," he said. "My dad keeps texting me."

I assured him it was okay. Once he put his phone away and brought his view back to the directions on my phone, I asked him if he and his dad were close.

"More so now. He's constantly texting and calling, sending me articles to read, links to videos. When I was little he was barely ever home."

I turned to look at him as we drove under a freeway overpass. His face turned from light to dark. I asked him what changed.

Rikesh explained that his parents came to the US from India with his infant sister two years before he was born. His father was hired as an engineer at Ford, where he became a workaholic. No longer occupied all day once he and his sister were in school, his mom grew bored and isolated. His father helped her get a data entry job in his building after she gained citizenship and was able to work. Over the years, her English improved and she transferred to an administrative assistant position. Now she was an executive assistant at headquarters, making more money than his father had when he was hired.

"My dad was laid off last spring," Rikesh said. "Now he has all these hobbies to occupy him. It's like he's trying to find himself." He laughed, but it was thin laughter.

I was surprised he hadn't told me about his family before, ashamed that I hadn't asked. I turned the knob on the radio. It went to static. I changed it back, decided to wait out the supermarket commercial.

"It's nice, though. Getting to know him better."

"Did you feel like you didn't know him before?" I asked.

Rikesh said his parents were worried he and his

sister would become too assimilated. He said they stopped speaking to his sister for six months after she got engaged to a white man. "They're all good now, though."

I could see him turn to face me in my peripheral vision. I changed lanes and passed a car full of old ladies. "So would your parents hate me?"

"They've made peace with the fact that I might not marry an Indian girl. That I want a love marriage. I'm pretty lucky that my sister paved the way for me."

I turned to him and we smiled at each other, sharing in the gratitude for his sister.

I noticed the flash of red brake lights in front of me and whipped my head forwards. I slammed on the brake. We lurched against our seatbelts, thunked back against our seats. The traffic ahead merged right to drive around a cop car. My heart was racing.

Rikesh put his hand on my knee. "We're okay," he said.

I tried to catch my breath. I switched into the right lane and slowly drove around the flashing lights of the police car, the rusted truck in front of it. I couldn't catch the face of the driver. It was too important that I look ahead.

The venue wasn't rustic at all. It looked like a resort. The ceremony was held in the clubhouse, in front of floor-to-ceiling windows overlooking the golf course. Beyond the golf course, I saw the barn: a pristine imitation of a barn, really. The sunshine made the dusting of snow atop its roof sparkle. Miri's mother, in a floor-length sequined gown, stopped us and pointed to it. This was where the reception would take place.

"Isn't it quaint?" she asked. It was a rich person's idea of quaint.

"I guess you're the more appropriately dressed one after all," I said to Rikesh after she'd left.

He held his elbow out to me. I hooked my arm in his and we followed the usher, a tuxedoed staff member, to our seats.

We were seated in the back. A string quartet played beside the altar. Now that I was still, my nerves caught up with me. I imagined what would have happened if I had hit that car. If I had hurt Rikesh. After the car accident in college, my mother insisted I start driving as soon as I was physically able. She didn't want me to develop a driving phobia. I tried to make the distinction in my mind. I tried not to let the association between cars and death loom constant. And, mostly, it worked. But tonight was one of those times when the accident came back to me. I took deep breaths. Tried the squared breathing technique. I watched the woman playing cello. Her eyes were closed. Her ability to remain in the moment, focused on her music, stabilized me here, too.

During the ceremony, I saw William in person for the first time. He looked at Miri lovingly. My attitude towards him softened as he cried through his vows.

They held hands and hugged after they exchanged words, before they were told to kiss. Rikesh reached for my hand. He brought it to his lap. He stroked my palm with his thumb. My whole body went limp.

There were heated golf carts to deliver guests to the barn. Rikesh and I decided to walk. I became happy with my choice to wear my cowboy boots, my wool tights, as we trekked down the winding road. I reached my arm out and wrapped it around his waist. A golf cart whizzed around us. The passengers' features were obscured by the plastic covering, so they were just multi-colored silhouettes. I pushed my shoulder into Rikesh's underarm. His body heat radiated through his suit jacket. His hand found my shoulder. He let out an exaggerated puff of air, so we could see a cloud of warm breath. I did the same. We alternated puffs. Rikesh started to make train chugging noises. I imitated a steam whistle. Another golf cart drove by and splashed a puddle of gray slush onto my boots. I jumped, startled, nearly shoving Rikesh over the curb. He grabbed my shoulders, steadying us, laughing at me. Then I joined in, great belly laughs simultaneously warming my insides and pulling icy air into my throat. I couldn't imagine Miri was any happier than I was in this moment.

Our table at the reception was between the dance floor and the buffet, directly in the line of traffic. Kaylee Sovinski was seated across from us. She didn't acknowledge me. She probably didn't recognize me. Or she didn't know how to speak to me without broaching the subject. Some people I'd run into from high school over the past few years started the conversation with a belated apology about the accident. Then we both felt awkward. This conversation would be easier after we'd had a few drinks, so I sucked down my cabernet and kept my vision downturned, kept my body angled towards Rikesh. But he was busy looking around the room, smiling and nodding at people he didn't know.

"We're up!" he said, delighted, and rose from the table.

As we walked through the buffet line, I looked for Miri. It was strange that I hadn't spoken to her yet. The wedding party's long table lined the dance floor perpendicular to the food. There was a crowd of people around the center of the table where Miri and William must have been seated, surrounded by their guests. Her mother was sitting at the edge of the group, looking up and nodding along with the conversation. On the other side of her, at the end of the table in his wheelchair, was Miri's grandfather. He held a fork of mashed potatoes parallel with the plate. His hand shook as he tried to maneuver them towards his mouth. He looked oblivious to the couple hundred people around him. He wore hearing aids but never turned them on properly. His vision was failing. The world was gradually shutting him out.

Rikesh nudged me, and I moved along in the line, adding greens to my plate. I sought out the smallest piece of chicken in the pan, scooping gravy on top of it.

After dinner, there were toasts. I watched Rikesh watch it all, politely and intently, as though he had any stock in Miri's cousin's anecdote about their childhood, acting out weddings with their dolls. He laughed when he was supposed to. It reminded me I should, too. Then came the first dance. Miri hadn't invited her father; William's mother used a walker, so he didn't dance with her. The two of them danced to Etta James.

I leaned towards Rikesh, my lips to his ear. "Do you want another drink?"

He shook his head and continued watching the couple.

I ordered a vodka tonic. I tried making small talk with the bartender, but he wouldn't engage. I leaned against the wall and watched the disco ball from afar, the flicker of lights. With my fingertips, cold and wet with condensation, I searched for the scar on my face. I couldn't find it. My fingers must have been numb. All over, I was starting to feel numb. It occurred to me that I'd probably just smeared my makeup. But it was dark, and it would be dark for the remainder of the night. I was feeling drunk. Blissfully, I realized, I didn't care about my face. Let it look ugly, I thought. The music changed to an up-tempo song that had been played at millions of weddings for the past thirty years. The DJ invited the other guests to the dance floor in that smarmy DJ voice where you could hardly pick out the words among all those elongated vowels. I drained my glass and asked the bartender for another. I made no effort to engage with him this time. But when he returned the glass without a lime, I shoved it back to him.

"I'd like a lime." I said. "And cherries, too!" I called over the music as he turned around.

He returned the glass and gave me a phony smile, the kind you get from wait staff when they're ready to turn around and complain about you to their co-workers. I rolled my eyes and took my drink.

I returned to our table. Only Rikesh and Kaylee were still seated. A slice of cake waited at my place setting. I noticed Kaylee had moved a seat closer to Rikesh. They were leaning towards each other, speaking over the empty seat between them.

"Wanna dance?" I grabbed his arm and set down my drink.

"Sure." He turned back to Kaylee and said something about it being nice talking to her. I yanked at his sleeve. I was ready to move my body, to have him all to myself. I pulled him onto the dance floor and grabbed his hands, swayed my hips. Ricky Martin was playing. Not a vast improvement from the last song, but at least it was something I could dance to.

Rikesh leaned to my ear, "She said she knew you from high school."

"Yeah?" I continued to dance around, but Rikesh

was mostly just shifting from one foot to the other.

"Why didn't you talk to her?" he asked.

"I assumed she didn't remember me. She didn't even acknowledge me. You, on the other hand," I raised my eyebrows. "She noticed you."

Rikesh scoffed. "She came alone. I was being friendly."

I nodded, stopped dancing. "Friendly," I repeated.

Rikesh stopped too. "You're being silly. Let's just dance." He held his forearms out to his side and shimmied his shoulders.

He was smiling like an idiot. I wanted to join him. I did. All around, there were people with their hands waving in the air, hair flipping, hips grinding. I wanted to have fun and feel free. His hands clasped my shoulders and shook them to the beat. I shrugged him away, headed for the bathroom.

Once the bathroom door closed I heard him knock.

"Whimsy?"

I paused just beyond the door, leaned my head against the wall and wept.

"Come out, please."

Two of Miri's coworkers were applying mascara in front of the gilded mirror. They passed the wand between one another. I'd never met them but I recognized them from photos on Miri's Facebook. They were in their bare feet, their heels strewn on the fainting couch beside them. Barns don't have wallpapered hallways. Barns don't have gilded mirrors and fainting couches in their bathrooms. We were in a fake barn filled with fake people. I turned back to the door.

He knocked again.

I wiped my eyes, tried to sound like I hadn't been crying. I wondered if I could go back out there and pretend I hadn't just stormed off the dance floor. Could I carry myself with such dignity? What I really wanted to do was return to the table, slap Kaylee across the face, pick up my piece of cake, and leave with Rikesh in arm. There was no way I could manage all three. I'd be lucky if I even found the cake hadn't yet been cleared.

Miri's coworkers walked past me, turning to their sides so they wouldn't bump me on their way out. When they pushed open the door, I could see Rikesh over their shoulders. He stood in the hallway, looking worried—or exasperated. I was afraid to find out which.

I stepped out to the hall. He wrapped his arms around me, and I shrank into a tiny egg in his loose grasp. I felt comforted thinking I could make this better when we were alone, when I could touch him, remind him how good we could be. He said he would take me home.

I thought he meant he was coming home with me.

Passing
Notes

I'd been menstruating for twelve days straight.

My mom said I needed to go to therapy more regularly. I'd been down to once a month for the past year. I told her I didn't like my therapist anymore. We'd run out of things to talk about. So she looked up a new clinician and made an appointment for me. I think my constant calls about Rikesh were depressing my mother. I reminded her that I hadn't wanted to hear about her relationship problems when I was growing up, either. She said she'd pay for the therapy.

It's not like I wanted to intentionally ruin her happiness.

He hadn't been returning my calls or texts.

School was busy. Progress reports were due, which meant I had to catch up on my grading. Parent-teacher conferences were at the end of the week. I needed to clean up my classroom, prepare a portfolio of work from each student to show off to their parents. I started going to the gym every day after school to work off my nerves. I tried to stay distracted.

On Tuesday, it had been a week and a half since I'd last seen him. I had an appointment with the new therapist in the evening. I stopped at the gym for a longer workout, braving the weight machines. I wanted to feel stronger.

In the locker room afterwards, I was peeling off my sweaty tank top when I heard two familiar voices. I wrapped myself in my towel and heard, "That was Miss Quinn!" I turned to see McKenzie and Jess, from my third period. They rounded the corner and exited the bathroom.

"Did you see her legs?" one of them said, the tiled alcove echoing. "She looks like Sasquatch!" The giggles trailed off.

I turned on the shower closest to me, stepped in, and closed the curtain. This was how students talked about their teachers, I told myself. It was how they got their entertainment. I remembered making fun of my own middle school teachers: my classmates and I tallied up the times Mrs. Wade cleared her throat in that disgusting, phlegmy way in history class; I had laughed when Henry squirted glue in my geometry teacher's coffee while he'd stepped out of the room. Still, I was angry. I looked down at my feet. A trail of red mixed with the swirl of water. I yanked out my tampon and flung it towards the trashcan. It thudded against the wall and slid into the can, leaving a streak of dark red on the white wall. I closed the curtain, pushed my head under the stream of water. I tried to cry but couldn't.

When I got out of the shower, I pulled my clothes over my wet skin, folded up my towel and set it on the floor under the hand dryer. I sat down on the towel and pressed the button to dry my hair. I watched the women entering and exiting the bathroom. Every sweating face nauseated me.

I skipped my appointment. I made up an excuse, emailed the therapist that I had gotten confused about the directions and showed up at the wrong office. Then I forwarded the email to my mother.

When I entered my classroom in the morning, the voicemail indicator on my phone was flashing red. McKenzie's mother had called, saying she couldn't make it to parent-teacher conferences that night.

"I need to have a discussion with you," she'd said, right before hanging up.

I rubbed the base of my skull where the throbbing was concentrated. The only thing worse than the run-in last night would be talking it over with her mother. I started to dial the number she'd left, but hung up. It was too early, and she'd probably called the night before. I listened to the message again, trying to decipher from her intonation if she wanted to talk about her daughter's grade or her talent for inflicting humiliation.

I waited until my planning period to call, when chances for interruption from students or co-workers were slimmest. I prayed for a voicemail; I'd simply give an overview of McKenzie's strengths and weaknesses, relay her current grade, and hope that that would suffice. Unfortunately, she picked up. I reminded myself to speak as though I were in a library. When I made my voice quieter, it naturally went down in pitch, so I sounded older. McKenzie's mother mostly dominated the conversation. She sounded over-caffeinated as she listed all of her daughter's extracurricular commitments and detailed her performance in past English classes.

"She's afraid she won't get into Honors English with her friends next year. What do you think? Maybe you can't say if you'll recommend her next year? Too soon? I'd understand."

"Well, she has a 78 percent right now."

"Oh, honey, we check the online grades every day. Do you think she needs a tutor?"

"Couldn't hurt."

Once third period began, McKenzie mostly avoided eye contact with me. She showed her friends a booklet of nail decals and asked their advice on which pattern to wear to the football game that weekend. I hit the tiny gong on my desk, which told the class to quiet down, that silent reading time had begun. I usually tried to read along with the students. I wanted to show solidarity, set an example that adults read even when they aren't forced to. I was reading *The Year of Magical Thinking*. Several times over the past two weeks, I'd gotten so sucked into the memoir I'd lose track of time until one of the students had the courage to say, "It's been over ten minutes, Miss Quinn." Today, I couldn't get into it. I kept looking at McKenzie to see if she was looking at me, teasing me in her head.

Her face remained hovering close to her book, *To All the Boys I've Loved Before*.

I looked at the clock and waited for ten minutes to pass. When it had, I directed the students to get out their copies of *Freak the Mighty*. The students journaled about the chapter we'd read the day before. I passed out new question sheets for the chapter we would read today. We went over the key vocabulary that would appear in the chapter, and the students copied down definitions of *tenement* and *evasive* and *depleted*. Then it was time to read. I had cups of popsicle sticks with each of the students' names on them. I chose one from the third period cup and asked Gavin to read aloud, while the other students followed along in their books. I walked around the room, reading silently and helping pronounce the words he stumbled on. I looked over shoulders, checking to make sure all of the students were on the right page and weren't just fake reading. It amazed me how many students were more entertained by their own imaginations than they were by the story in front of them.

We got through five pages, read by five different students when I noticed Jess reach towards the window beside her. She was seated two desks ahead of McKenzie. I saw her scribbling on a piece of paper, laid inside of her book, then quietly fold the paper up, and set it back on the windowsill. Moments later, McKenzie reached towards the sill and snatched the note. I kept pacing, but rounded the opposite side of the classroom so I could watch as they continued their operation. McKenzie unfolded the note and wrote a message as she grinned. *Those little bitches are writing about me*, I thought. My teeth clenched tight. I finally noticed Kelsey had stopped reading. We had finished the page. I returned to the desk and drew another popsicle stick. "Destiny, you're up." I said. By this time, Jess was writing on the paper. I stood at the front of the room, feigning reading, and waited for her to replace the note on the windowsill. When she did, I took long strides to reach it. I intercepted, swiping up the note before McKenzie could reach it. McKenzie threw me a look of disgust.

"What's this?" I said, holding the folded square of lined paper up.

"Nothing!" she said, eyes wide.

"If you focused on the lessons instead of notes, McKenzie, you might not need a tutor to get a decent grade." I turned around and walked back to my desk. I noticed students shifting in their seats, gathering their things. It was almost the end of class. The students always noticed before I did. I examined the clean stack of detention slips on my desk. The bell rang. I just set the note down next to the slips.

McKenzie huffed out of the room and slammed the classroom door behind her. She was a smart girl. She knew how to make a statement of protest without risking punishment. My moment of triumph quickly faded into discomfort. I wanted her to like me. I wanted all my students to like me.

As my next class arrived, I sat at my desk and unfolded the note. It was a series of single sentences in alternating handwriting. I scanned it first, looking for my name. Not seeing it, I read each statement carefully. A conversation about the indoor soccer team, whose parent would pick them up after practice, and what they would eat for dinner.

Conferences

Parent-teacher conferences lasted four hours. I had a line of parents the entire time, so it went by quickly. I got into the rhythm of showing each parent their child's portfolio, giving some suggestions and a compliment, then handing the parent a grade sheet to signal the end of the conversation.

A handful of parents brought their children with them. One, Brody, sat curled in on himself, so different from his usual posture and demeanor: stretched out, cracking jokes. His father spoke to him too close, threateningly. My vision went to the man's belt line, then to his son's arms and face. I tried to be overly positive about Brody, said he contributed to group discussions readily, that he was a positive member of the classroom who created a sense of community among his peers. The fact that the bonding occurred at my expense, or the expense of his classmates, no longer seemed relevant. His father turned to Brody and said in a booming voice, "That's good. Good boy."

Even the encouragement sounded aggressive.

The other English teachers, four women with suspiciously similar pixie cuts, invited me to get post-conference drinks. I was exhausted from the hours of composure, speaking with a forced sense of authority.

But I'd heard the ways they described other teachers who declined their invitations to lunch or drinks. Rejecting the offer was asking them to gossip about you.

Lucinda was both the social leader and the department chair. She had been teaching 8th grade English for almost thirty years. Her slogan as a teacher was, "Don't smile until Christmas." I thought it just applied in the classroom, but I didn't think she'd ever smiled at me, either. Her students complained about her incessantly: the homework, the harsh grading, the strict rules. Yet she was the only teacher who had former students visit her classroom on a regular basis. This was the only time I saw her look happy, when I passed by her room after school and she was speaking with a high school student who'd come for advice on college applications or to thank her for preparing them for their high school essays. She had their respect. I both hated her for not being nicer to me—not offering, as the most veteran member of our department, to support the new teacher—and admired her. I watched her. I attempted to mimic her ways, but the kids just laughed at me when I tried being stern.

Lucinda ordered a burger with a lettuce wrap instead of a bun and a vodka soda. I'd never seen her eat carbs or sugar. The restraint she exhibited in the classroom seemed to carry outside of it, too. The other teachers ordered wine. When the server got to me, I asked for a beer, and he just stared at me.

"A pint, please," I repeated, like he had been waiting for me to specify the size.

"Can I see some ID?"

The women all cooed about how young I was, how adorable that I'd been carded. I could feel my cheeks redden as he handed my license back and I slipped it into my wallet. I looked up and caught Lucinda's attention. She winked at me. I took my jacket off and relaxed into my chair. I listened as Wendy discussed her daughter's new boyfriend, a former student of hers, and she complained that she couldn't forget how he'd been a serial bra-snapper in middle school.

"He seems okay now. I mean, it was three years ago. Now he's rifling through my fridge, in my daughter's bedroom. Every time he comes over I just keep picturing what a little creep he used to be."

The artichoke dip Wendy had ordered arrived and she offered to share. I dug in, starving but too cheap to order food. I gulped my beer and felt better, calmer. Lucinda added that sexual harassment at a young age said more about his father than him. Gabby scoffed and said that was unfair. She didn't feel she should be blamed for every stupid thing her children did.

I was drained. I had been "on" for nearly twelve hours. I no longer had the energy to feign interest in someone else's problems. I couldn't muster anything thoughtful to contribute. I sipped my beer and looked out the windows.

In my mind, every dark-haired man of a tall,

slightly hunched, stature was Rikesh. Which is why I doubted myself when I thought I noticed him walking hand-in-hand with another woman on the street. Then they turned into the restaurant. It really was Rikesh. And I knew the woman—Jane. I'd spent enough time studying photos I'd found of her online. Her profile picture was an image of her seated under a tree with a spider monkey on her shoulder, her face scrunched and giggling. As they entered and approached the hostess' stand, his eyes met mine and he quickly averted his view. They were led towards the back of the restaurant. I watched Jane in the few seconds I had before they slipped through the crowd by the bar and were seated out of my view. She had blonde hair, bluntly cut at her chin. She wore those cheap cloth Mary Janes, a turquoise t-shirt, and no traces of makeup. Everything about her gave the impression of an overgrown six-year-old, except for her chest. I looked at the door and wondered how soon I could escape. I looked back in their direction, trying to catch sight of them again. Only snatches of their seated figures: her shoulder as a waiter pushed through the crowd, the top of his gelled hair when I lifted myself up in my seat. The women were complaining about their husbands now. I finished the rest of my beer. I asked the waiter for my bill. I explained to the women that I needed to get to bed. They made those cooing sounds again.

In the morning, I tried to make myself waffles. They were the frozen kind you just put in the toaster, but I burned them anyway. I had tucked my phone at the bottom of my dresser drawer so I would stop looking at it. Just as I began to detect the burning smell, my phone rang. I opened the dresser and moved aside my sweaters. *Rikesh* lit up the screen.

"Oh, fuck you," I said and slammed the drawer shut. I immediately opened it back up, stared at it. It was still ringing. I picked it up.

"Hey," he said, like there was nothing out of the ordinary.

I waited a few moments to see what he'd say. I'd be damned if I was the one to initiate this conversation. "Yes?" I finally said.

He asked me to meet for brunch. I hated how he said brunch: both the way he pronounced it and the fact that he used the term at all. *Men shouldn't say 'brunch,'* I thought.

I chose the Big Bagel Deli because it was inconvenient for him, in an overcrowded suburb I'd heard him complain about having to drive through for a Free Press assignment. I didn't like it that much either; I didn't want our conversation, and the memory of it, to taint another one of my favorite places. I'd craved Japanese food over the past few weeks—soothing miso soup and ginger to settle my stomach. But I couldn't bring myself to go back to the restaurant where we first ate together.

At the deli, I ordered an egg bagel sandwich and coffee. He ordered the same thing and paid for us both. His movements seemed stiff. There was a sadness about him. Though I wasn't sure if I just wanted him to seem sad.

We stood by the counter as a teenage boy made our sandwiches. He presented them on a single tray. Rikesh picked it up, carried it to the center of the room. I held our coffees. They scalded my hands. The boy had forgotten to give us those protective jackets. Rikesh turned around and asked where I wanted to sit. He gave a half-smile, like he was asking for permission to smile all the way. I remained stone-faced and sat at a table in the corner. He set the tray down and pushed a plate in front of me. I watched him stuff his bagel awkwardly in his mouth.

"So who was that?" I took the lid off my coffee, set it on the table, and allowed the steam to escape.

He held up one finger while he chewed.

"Was it Jane?" I realized I didn't want to hear him say her name. "You can just nod or shake your head."

He began nodding, swallowed, and then took a sip of his coffee.

I looked at my sandwich: slimy tomato, slick mayo, shiny yellow egg patty, pale bagel. I removed the top half and tore the bread into bits on my plate, like I was preparing to feed them to a duck. I popped a piece in my mouth and chewed. "So she's back."

"I wasn't expecting it." He wiped a trace of mayonnaise from the corner of his lips. "She had some medical issues, and she had to leave Lesotho early."

"I get it." What I'd wanted to scream was: *I don't give a shit about her issues*. I smashed a piece of bagel between my fingers and rolled it into a doughy ball. "She's attractive."

"We have a history."

I said, "And she's not deformed."

Rikesh straightened in his seat. His guilt-stricken look sharpened into something more determined and self-assured. "It's not that you have scars—it's that you're obsessed with them. I don't know if you were always like this, but it's your narcissism that bothers me." He looked out the window and scoffed. "Your thinking is so defective. People have acne more noticeable than what's on your face."

I looked to the window. It was broad daylight out. No reflection was detectable.

After a few moments, staring, detached, I saw Rikesh rise in my peripheral vision. He collected napkins from the table, his and mine, too, and placed them on his plate. I got up with my plate of partially eaten food, full cup of coffee. I saw that teenage boy behind the counter sitting, hunched over on a stool, staring open-mouthed at his phone.

Rikesh returned the tray to the shelf above the trash can. I shoved my plate into the trash. "I see what you're doing, you know," I said.

He was walking towards the exit, but he stopped and turned around.

"You used me." My voice was shaking. I took a

moment to gain strength. "You'd never given up hope that Jane would take you back. And now you're trying to make yourself feel less guilty about it."

Rikesh took a step further from me. He stared at the floor. At first I thought he was considering the truth in my accusation. But when he looked up at me, I knew that wasn't the case at all. He felt sorry for me.

"*I'm* a narcissist? So are *you*. So is *everybody*."

Rikesh put his hand on the glass door beside him. His lips parted like he was going to reply. Instead, he exhaled. Then he turned, pushed the door open, and left.

Bodily
Expressions

Every December, the school held a concert featuring the band, orchestra, and choir classes. The art classes displayed their calligraphy and modeling clay pieces in the lobby outside of the auditorium. Judith agreed to let the Bodily Expressions Club perform dance numbers between the band and choir performances. After much debate over whether we wanted to be seen as modern or interpretive dancers, we settled on the club name. Everyone would get to choose their own songs. We lost Alvin after the second rehearsal. When I asked his sister in my third period why he'd quit, she said all his friends were in Minecraft club. His loss was restored by Gia's new recruits. The four eighth graders now made up the majority of the club. I was relieved that she and Torrey hadn't bailed, too; it was because of them that our group remained in existence and, though still small, had some much-needed cachet.

Gia and her crew choreographed a group routine to a top forty song called "Glitter Revival." Stephanya developed a piece to a song by a Scandinavian death metal band I hadn't heard before. She insisted it was on the radio all the time. The students who would perform in the showcase were excused from their afternoon classes for the dress rehearsal. I pretended

I didn't see Judith when I walked down the carpeted auditorium aisles. On stage, the band was finishing up their rendition of "Silver Bells." A reedy squeak accented the melody. The band teacher motioned to stop, then ordered the clarinet section to fix their mistakes. I called the dance club to huddle up and gave my best shot at a pep talk. Torrey's eyes wandered onto the stage. She smiled and waved to someone in the percussion section.

"*Listen*, guys. I just want to tell you I'm really proud of all your hard work. It's okay to be nervous. You're more courageous than I would have ever been at your age. You can do this. Know that your self-expression will help inspire your classmates and give them permission to do the same. You're accomplishing something really—"

"Miss Quinn," Torrey interrupted. "They're packing up the band."

"Something really important!" I said quickly. I turned Stephanya by her shoulders and gave her back a light pat to urge her forward. I was worried for her. I prayed none of the students would holler cruelties up to the stage as she danced. The other girls stood at the wings of the stage as Stephanya took her place.

Judith's voice came over the PA system. "Please welcome the first performance from our Bodily Expressions Club, Stephanya Waters dancing to... 'Black Candelabra' by, uh, Blood Celibate."

The music blared through the speakers. Stephanya

had been incredible during the practices in the weeks leading up to the dress rehearsal. But on the stage, she seemed to wither under the heat of the spotlights. It highlighted the curve of the back of her neck. She'd cut her hair short the week before. Now it stuck out on top of her head like a hedgehog, pointing in front of her as her face hung towards the floor. I worried she'd fall; her center of gravity was so tilted. But she did her usual twirls and moves. When it was over I unclenched, tried to lower my shoulders and breathe. My armpits had grown damp. She ambled off the stage, without the bow we had rehearsed, and plunked herself in a seat on the edge of the third row. As Gia's group was introduced, I sat down near Stephanya.

"You did a good job, Steph," I said, quietly. She pulled her knees to her chest and shoved her head down between them.

I watched the girls dance on stage to the bubblegum music. I kept taking quick glances at Stephanya. She remained in a ball. By the end of the song, she raised her head, clapped for her teammates. They exited the stage and joined us in the seats. Finally, Maureen went onstage and danced to a country song, adding the hand claps that I'd insisted she cut.

When the dress rehearsal was over, the students were sent back to catch the last half of their 5th period. I had a substitute in my room, so I hung back and helped the art teacher label the pieces on display. Judith found me trying to reassemble a purple clay snowman I'd accidentally knocked over.

"What did you think of your girls' performances?"

I held my hands out beside the snowman, waiting to make sure it wouldn't teeter again, ready to catch it. When it stayed upright, I turned to Judith. "They did great."

"Hmmm."

"What? What's wrong?" The snowman fell again. I shoved the head back on, smooshing his hat sideways in the process.

"I'm concerned about Stephanya's song. It's kind of scary, don't you think?"

"*Scary?* She's thirteen. A lot of kids like that music." My neck muscles tightened.

"The problem is, this is a *holiday* show."

"It's what she wanted to dance to." I picked up my remaining stack of labels. I couldn't look at her anymore. The desire for violence would be too great.

"I thought you would have had better judgment."

I copied down a student's name and attached it to a pencil drawing of Lil Wayne. I tried to devise an argument in my head.

"You need to pull her number." Judith stood there, waiting for my acknowledgement.

"Oh-kay." I kept my gaze on the labels in my hands until she walked away.

I stopped in the library before returning to my classroom. I looked up Stephanya's schedule. She was in algebra. I headed to her classroom, sticky note in hand. I opened the door slowly and slipped into the classroom. Ken was announcing the students' homework. I scanned the room and spotted her desk along the front row. I tried to be quiet, but all the students watched me as I approached.

"Sorry, I'm just going to—" I pointed to her, then set the note on her desk. *See me after class.*

The sub tried to report back to me about the afternoon classes. He complained about my fourth period.

"Those children are insane." He rubbed under his nose with the side of his pointer finger.

"Yeah. Thanks a lot." I slipped behind him to reclaim my desk. I didn't really care how it went; I'd learned quickly not to expect my students to get anything done with a substitute teacher in the room.

He packed up his briefcase slowly. I logged onto my computer and tried to look busy. I glanced at the note he'd written me on my desk, on top of the attendance rosters: a report on each class with the names of the students who misbehaved. He'd written his name and contact information at the bottom should I need him to sub again.

"You take care now," he said and left the room.

"Would you close the door, please?" I asked.

The door slammed shut.

Moments later, it opened again. Stephanya came in, stooped under the weight of her backpack. She wore a sparkly red scarf and a black snow jacket with a large fur-trimmed hood—the kind of jacket she might have inherited from her grandmother.

"Is the rest of the club coming?" She sat in her usual lunchtime seat. I tried to determine her mood, if she'd recovered. With her reconstructed cleft lip, it was difficult for me to tell if she was frowning, and her eyes always looked the same, round and watery. I'd never seen her cry, though. I imagined she leaked out all her tears throughout the day, like routine maintenance.

"Just you," I said. I got up from my desk and came closer to her, to the table nearby where I kept copies of daily assignments.

"What's wrong?" she mumbled.

I began to cry. I turned my head away to wipe my eyes.

"What is it?"

When I looked up at her face, so earnest and concerned, I began sobbing. I hunched over and covered my face.

"Are you okay?" She began to get up from her desk.

"No, I'm fine. Sit back down. *Please*." I smeared my face with my sleeve and tried to breathe. "Stephanya, I have some bad news." I bit my lip and looked at the poster on the wall behind her. It read: *Today is a great day to learn something new!* I'd found it rolled up in the classroom closet at the beginning of the year.

I sighed. "You can't dance your piece in the showcase."

She looked up at the ceiling. Her shoulders rose and fell slowly.

I moved closer and squatted down beside her desk. "They're just not ready for you. They don't get it." I waited for her to look at me. When she wouldn't acknowledge me, I began to tear up again.

She turned her head slowly and shrugged. "I'm sort of relieved. I don't want to dance anymore."

I raised up from my haunches. She got up from her desk and pulled the straps of her backpack over her baggy coat.

I was ready to argue, to tell her it was no reason to quit, but I just nodded, tapped my fingers against the table. I sniffed back the snot threatening to emerge from my nostrils. "Well, you can focus on your poetry now."

She mumbled inaudibly.

"Have a good night, Stephanya."

She disappeared from the room.

I hadn't looked closely at this back corner of the room lately. The floor was covered in pencil shavings. The desks were covered in gum and anatomical graffiti. Even kids marked their territory.

Testing

Spring is standardized testing season. All the teachers complain about losing valuable time in the classroom, but I'm grateful for a respite from preparing lessons. All I have to do is distribute pencils, read the directions someone else wrote, and collect the tests in an envelope for a machine somewhere far away to scan. In my newly free evenings, I am learning to cook. On Friday, we wrap up the final section of state testing. My mother and Barb are coming over for dinner before going to see some foreign film at the art theater nearby.

I stop at the grocery store on my way home to pick up ingredients. Barb is always trying new supplements and diets. My mother says her doctors failed her and she is searching for her own cure. Now, she is gluten free. I found a recipe for a pizza with a crust made from cauliflower. I try to find prosciutto to put on top for my mom. I thought I would make my own sauce, but by the time I am pushing the cart through these fluorescent-lit hallways exhaustion hits me. I pick up a can of organic pizza sauce. I search for hormone-free mozzarella. The only variety they have is the fresh kind, for eight dollars. I consider deeming it a vegan pizza so I can skip the cheese, skip the meat, save some money. But I want it to taste good. I want to impress them. I plop the cheese into my cart, find the prosciutto.

I round the corner to the produce department. I hear a familiar ringtone that makes me flinch. I've overheard it a few times over the past months, from a neighboring table at a taco place once, from a nearby purse at the mall another time. It's the piccolo-like trilling I'd set for Rikesh's calls. I stop my cart and look around. No one is close enough. I sling my purse in front of me, resting it in the children's seat, and dig around. It gets louder. I feel the vibration. In my hand, the caller's name is confirmed. The noise of computer-simulated woodwind competes with an unintelligible announcement over the intercom. The vibration shoots through my forearm. I cradle it in my fingers for a moment, reliving the feelings of the previous fall: the thrill of seeing his name on my phone, the flip of my stomach, the glee. It stops ringing. My cart nudges to one side.

"I'm so sorry." An old woman's smoker voice startles me. She tries to pull her cart back, but it won't move. Her wheel is stuck.

"It's okay." I switch my phone to silent, drop it in my purse, and back up my cart. I go the long way around the table of bananas to reach the vegetables. The cauliflower display looks newly stocked. There are three pristine rows of plastic-wrapped heads in white, green, and purple varieties.

• • •

"You know you're welcome to come with us, Whimsy," Barb tells me. "We can pay for your ticket." She helps herself to another slice of pizza. It has turned out crumbly, an odd consistency. I'm grateful I loaded it with cheese.

"It's okay."

Barb and Mom repeat how much they loved the dinner. They are mostly just trying to be encouraging. It is only six-thirty, but it's getting dark out. The light from above the dinner table is almost blinding by comparison. I am surprised my mom was willing to make the trip here tonight. She doesn't like driving home in the dark. I wipe pizza sauce from the corner of my lip. I return my hand to my face. It feels smoother than usual, almost like normal skin.

"It seems like my scars are smoothing out," I say, eyes still fixated on the blackness outside.

Mom smacks her lips together as she chews, as she's done for as long as I can remember. She leans toward me, squinting. "Looks the same to me," she says.

"Hmm." Barb's gaze flickers between my mother and me.

"Sorry, sweetie," my mother adds.

It feels too quiet after they've left. There are crumbs on the counter, bits of food on the floor. I put on a podcast about black holes and alternate universes, run a sponge under the faucet and wipe the table. I wonder why Rikesh called me, if he is still with Jane. He didn't leave a voicemail. I'm trying to resist the gnawing urge to call back. I want to know what he would have said. I shake the crumbs from the sponge into the sink. I notice something black along the edge and wipe it. I crush it, examine the sponge's underside: an ant.

For a short period, it was like this: I would think of him and he would call. I thought it a telepathic connection. I go to my bedroom and check my phone. One missed call and one voicemail—Rikesh again.

I play the message and hear his voice as I haven't heard it before. He is struggling for breath between words, nearly hyperventilating, hysterical. He says he needs to talk. He says he doesn't know why I'm not picking up. For once, I don't take the time to dissect his words. His tone has me panicked.

"Whimsy?" he sounds a little calmer, but his voice is still soft, vulnerable.

"What's wrong?"

"Can I come over?"

After hanging up, I pull the bedspread up over my sheets. I wipe the toothpaste from the bathroom mirror. I think, *These are the things I should be doing anyway.*

He's gotten a haircut since I saw him last—short all over now. From the bottom of the stairs his facial expression mirrors his voice. I recognize his shirt, though: maroon, collared. And while he's still making his way up the stairs, I know the material has tiny maroon flowers stitched all over, creating a texture I can see when my face is resting against his chest. When he reaches the doorway, I don't know whether to hug him. I open the door further and hide my body behind it so I don't have to decide. Rikesh grabs the handle and shuts the door, pulls me towards him. He sobs, and I feel my cheek push into the bumpy fabric.

He doesn't tell me what's wrong. This is how I know it's Jane.

"Lie down," I say, pointing to the bed.

He falls on top of the covers. His shoes hang off the edge of the mattress, one lace untied.

I go to the bathroom and grab a washcloth. I run the water until it's frigid, then hold the cloth underneath. I fold up the damp cloth into a rectangle. In my bedroom, Rikesh has stopped sobbing, but I see the sheen of tears against his cheekbones. As I approach, he closes his eyes. I cover his forehead and eyelids with the cloth. We are both silent. The usual noises from the downtown street are absent, too. It's like the world is on mute. I sit at the edge of the bed, my hip barely touching his abdomen. I watch his chest. His breathing slows. I get up and return to the bathroom. I find the vial of flower essences in the medicine cabinet. It is supposed to be a natural stress reliever. This is the only time, in my memory, that I am calm in his presence.

"Open your mouth and lift your tongue," I say,

standing above him, squeezing the dropper.

He hesitates, then follows my instructions. I place several drops on the rosy spot behind his lower teeth. He closes his mouth and scrunches his lips. The amber concoction contains alcohol as a preservative. I'm not sure if the calming effects come from the flowers or a psychosomatic response to the sting of alcohol. I touch a white button on his shirt. Then another. I circle the plastic with my finger.

I tell myself it's time to move away. From the couch I watch him lying there. After a few minutes, he lifts his arm and pulls off the cloth, wipes his face with his palms.

"Thank you," he says to the ceiling. "That's just what I needed."

Rikesh pushes himself up. When he looks at me, he smiles, embarrassed. I don't return it. I'm not going to give him absolution. He nods like he understands and opens the door. I hear his footsteps descending, an uneven clomping, like he's skipping down. It's familiar, already nostalgic.

At the kitchen window, I pull back the curtain. The lights of his car flash twice as he unlocks it. I hear the beep. Under the interior light he sits at the wheel and leans back to one side, reaching, reclining his seat. After a while, the cabin darkens. Now there is just the reflection of the streetlight on the hood of his car. I let go of the curtain, return to washing the last of the dishes. The caulking at the edge of the sink has split;

there is a whole line of tiny ants marching out of the opening. They'll get the crumbs I've left behind. I take the rough side of the sponge and wipe them away, rinse the sponge. The ants disappear down the drain.

As I get ready for bed I notice the wrinkles in the comforter where his body made its mark. I look out the window one more time. His car is still there.

When I wake up, it takes several moments to remember last night, to separate sleep from the surreal time he spent in my apartment again. I get out of bed and look out the window. His car is gone. A cable truck sits in its place.

Acknowledgments

I want to express my gratitude to Bryan Hurt with *Joyland Magazine*, Helen McClory with *Necessary Fiction*, and Alan Good and DeMisty D. Bellinger with *Malarkey Books* for previously publishing sections of this novella in slightly different forms. Thank you to my friends & family who read and gave feedback on this manuscript or parts of it: Michal Dvir, Phoebe Rusch, Elizabeth Ellen, Brad King, Noel Anson, Horam Kim, Amanda McNeil, Rebecca van Laer, Samantha McLeod, and Josh Mound (thank you, Josh, for encouraging my writing, always). Thank you Tim Kinsella for choosing *Whimsy* as the winner of the Wild Onion Novella Contest. Enormous gratitude goes to Joshua Bohnsack and Joe Demes, the talented and dedicated editors who worked wonders on this manuscript. Thank you to the rest of the team at Long Day Press. I'm so grateful you've made this book possible. And thank you—*thank you*—dear reader.

Shannon McLeod is the author of the essay chapbook *Pathetic* (Etchings Press 2016). Her writing has appeared in *Tin House*, *Prairie Schooner*, *Hobart*, and *SmokeLong Quarterly*, among other publications. Born in Detroit, she now lives in Virginia where she teaches high school English. You can find Shannon on her website at www.shannon-mcleod.com.

Long Day Press

New & Forthcoming Titles

Love Stories & Other Love Stories
Justin Brouckaert
Stories
ISBN: 9781950987115 • $14

On the Campaign Trail
J. Bradley
Novella
ISBN: 9781950987047 • $10

What's On the Menu?
Chase Griffin
Novella
ISBN: 9781950987016 • $14

The Everys
Cody Lee
Screenplay
ISBN: Forthcoming • $TBA

LongDayPress.com   @LongDayPress